Y0-ABZ-157

Did Matt think she was sexy?

Shawn continued to mull it over. And she finally admitted to herself that she was drawn to Matt, and not just because he'd been kind and concerned about her daughter. Shawn would have liked him even if she'd met him somewhere else, under different circumstances.

But, she thought regretfully, he really *was* too young for her. Her friends might think ten years was nothing, but Shawn knew better. When he was forty, in the prime of his life, she'd be fifty, heading downhill.

No, it would never work.

Besides, he wasn't interested in her.

End of story.

Dear Reader,

So—it's the new year. Time for new beginnings. And we at Special Edition take that very seriously, so this month we offer the first of six books in our new FAMILY BUSINESS continuity. In it, a family shattered by tragedy finds a way to rebuild. *USA TODAY* bestselling author Susan Mallery opens the series with *Prodigal Son,* in which the son who thought he'd rid himself of the family business is called back to save it—with the help of his old (figuratively speaking) and beautiful business school nemesis. Don't miss it!

It's time for new beginnings for reader favorite Patricia Kay also, who this month opens CALLIE'S CORNER CAFÉ, a three-book miniseries centered around a small-town restaurant that serves as home base for a group of female friends. January's kickoff book in the series is *A Perfect Life,* which features a woman who thought she had the whole life-plan thing down pat—until fate told her otherwise. Talk about reinventing yourself! Next up, Judy Duarte tells the story of a marriage-phobic man, his much-married mother…and the wedding planner who gets involved with them both, in *His Mother's Wedding.* Jessica Bird continues THE MOOREHOUSE LEGACY with *His Comfort and Joy.* For years, sweet, small-town Joy Moorehouse has fantasized about arrogant, big-city Grayson Bennett…. Are those fantasies about to become reality? In *The Three-Way Miracle* by Karen Sandler, three people—a woman, a man and a child—greatly in need of healing, find all they need in each other. And in Kate Welsh's *The Doctor's Secret Child,* what starts out as a custody battle for a little boy turns into a love story. You won't be able to put it down….

Enjoy them all—and don't forget next month! It's February, and you know what that means….

Here's to new beginnings….

Gail Chasan
Senior Editor

Please address questions and book requests to:
Silhouette Reader Service
U.S.: 3010 Walden Ave., P.O. Box 1325, Buffalo, NY 14269
Canadian: P.O. Box 609, Fort Erie, Ont. L2A 5X3

A PERFECT LIFE
PATRICIA KAY

SPECIAL EDITION®
Published by Silhouette Books
America's Publisher of Contemporary Romance

If you purchased this book without a cover you should be aware that this book is stolen property. It was reported as "unsold and destroyed" to the publisher, and neither the author nor the publisher has received any payment for this "stripped book."

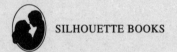

SILHOUETTE BOOKS

ISBN 0-373-24730-3

A PERFECT LIFE

Copyright © 2006 by Patricia A. Kay

All rights reserved. Except for use in any review, the reproduction or utilization of this work in whole or in part in any form by any electronic, mechanical or other means, now known or hereafter invented, including xerography, photocopying and recording, or in any information storage or retrieval system, is forbidden without the written permission of the editorial office, Silhouette Books, 233 Broadway, New York, NY 10279 U.S.A.

All characters in this book have no existence outside the imagination of the author and have no relation whatsoever to anyone bearing the same name or names. They are not even distantly inspired by any individual known or unknown to the author, and all incidents are pure invention.

This edition published by arrangement with Harlequin Books S.A.

® and ™ are trademarks of Harlequin Books S.A., used under license. Trademarks indicated with ® are registered in the United States Patent and Trademark Office, the Canadian Trade Marks Office and in other countries.

Visit Silhouette Books at www.eHarlequin.com

Printed in U.S.A.

PATRICIA KAY,

formerly writing as Trisha Alexander, is the *USA TODAY* bestselling author of more than thirty contemporary romances. She lives in Houston, Texas. To learn more about her, visit her Web site at www.patriciakay.com.

Prologue

Maple Hills, Ohio
Early January

Courage, Shawn Fletcher told herself. *Courage.*

She poured a cup of coffee and eyed the clock on the kitchen wall. It was almost nine. Lauren, Shawn's fifteen-year-old daughter, would be home soon from her sleepover. Shawn took a deep, shaky breath.

The next hour or two would be among the hardest Shawn had ever faced. And that was really saying something, because the past few months had contained more shocks and stunning blows than any one person should have to endure. Starting with the agonizing news of her parents' deaths in October and ending with the discovery of her husband's cheating, Shawn's entire life had been turned upside down.

Please, God, please give me the strength to tell Lauren about this new loss in a way that won't devastate her. Or drive us apart just when we need each other most.

But even as Shawn silently formed the prayer, she knew her daughter would not receive this news well. How could she? *Her* entire life would be turned upside down, too. And in many ways, what was going to happen now would be harder for Lauren to bear than it would be for Shawn.

Sighing, Shawn walked to the window over the sink and slowly drank her coffee. There'd been a fresh snowfall this morning, and the yard glistened under the late-afternoon sun. She watched as a rusty-looking fox squirrel scampered up one of the maple trees that dotted the side yard. Many of her neighbors hated squirrels, but their antics amused Shawn, and she encouraged them to visit by putting ears of corn out every morning as well as birdseed for the cardinals, finches and bluebirds prevalent in the village. She was like her mother that way. Margaret Gibson had loved all animals. She hadn't even minded the occasional gopher who had dug tunnels in her backyard.

Oh, Mom, I miss you and Dad so much.

Tears pooled in Shawn's eyes, and she swallowed against the lump in her throat. Her parents had only been in their early sixties. They should have had at least twenty more years to enjoy their lives. If it hadn't been for that out-of-control bus driver…

But no amount of wishing would change what had happened. Shawn's beloved parents were gone. And she would have to learn to live without them. Just as she would have to learn to live without her husband.

As her mind filled again with thoughts of Lauren and the ordeal ahead, a dark SUV rounded the corner at the end of the street and approached their house, stopping at the foot of the driveway. A moment later, Lauren climbed out of the back. Shawn's pulse quickened as she watched Lauren wave goodbye to her friend Heather, then walk up the driveway. Spying her mother in the window, Lauren waved, and the innocence in her grin made Shawn's heart constrict.

Oh, sweetheart, Shawn thought, *if only I could keep that smile on your face. If only I could keep you sheltered from this ugliness.*

But all the *if onlys* in the world wouldn't change the facts. Nor would they soften the blow Lauren was about to receive.

"Hi, Mom!" Lauren called out as she entered the mudroom off the kitchen.

Shawn heard the clump of Lauren's clogs being kicked off. She swallowed hard. Lauren was such a good kid. She didn't deserve this. Then again, did any kid deserve a broken home?

"Hi, sweetie," Shawn said when Lauren walked into the kitchen. "Did you have fun at Heather's?"

"Yeah, it was great!" Lauren's wildly curly blond hair—the exact duplicate of Shawn's when she was her age—was pulled back into a messy ponytail, and her blue eyes looked tired. But her voice vibrated with enthusiasm. "We watched the whole first two seasons of *Friends* on DVD and gave each other pedicures and ate tons of popcorn and talked about boys and clothes." She grinned. "And Heather's mother made those brownies for us the way we like 'em—with those butterscotch chips in them—and we had Sloppy Joes and by the time we finally went to bed, we were, like, so stuffed!"

Shawn smiled, even though inside her stomach was churning.

Lauren plopped down onto a kitchen chair. "Where's Dad? Did he go into the office?" She grabbed a banana from the ceramic fruit bowl in the middle of the kitchen table and began to peel it. "I'm starving."

"Didn't you eat breakfast before you left Heather's?"

Lauren made a face. "I don't like eggs." She took a bite of the banana.

Shawn's heart started pounding again. This was it. She couldn't avoid it another moment. "Lauren," she began, "sweetheart…there's, um, something I need to tell you about Dad."

Lauren continued eating her banana. "Did he have to go on *another* business trip? Jeez, Mom. I hate it when he's gone so much."

Oh, God. Shawn pulled out a chair across from her daughter and sat down. Her stomach felt as if someone were tap-dancing inside. She wet her lips. "No, um, that's not exactly it." Shawn took a deep breath. This was going to be even harder than she'd thought. "Honey, look, I'm sure you're aware that things have been kind of strained between your father and me lately."

Lauren frowned. For the first time, she seemed to sense that what Shawn had to say might not be routine Mom-talk.

"Anyway, we, um…we talked last night and, um…we've come to a decision." Shawn took another deep breath. "Dad and I are getting a divorce."

Lauren just stared at her.

"I'm sorry, sweetie, I know this is a blow, but—"

Lauren jumped up, hitting the table in the process and causing the ceramic fruit bowl to bounce. "A divorce! What do you *mean,* things have been strained? What…what are you *talking* about?" Tears welled in her eyes, and she shook her head back and forth.

"Sweetie, I'm sorry…"

"Where *is* Dad? Where *is* he?"

"I—I don't know. He left last night."

"No!" Lauren cried, putting her hands over her ears.

"No!" The tears overflowed, rolling down her face. "You *can't* get a divorce!"

"Honey…" Shawn wanted to cry herself. But tears were a luxury she couldn't afford this morning. For Lauren's sake she had to stay in control. Getting up, Shawn walked around the table and tried to put her arms around Lauren, but Lauren pushed her away.

"Why are you doing this?" she sobbed. "Why are you divorcing Daddy?"

"Lauren, I…" But what could Shawn say? She certainly couldn't tell Lauren the truth. *Honey, last night when I came home from Grandma and Grandpa's house, I finally found out just who your father has been screwing for the past year.* "Sometimes adults just… they just find they can't live together anymore. It doesn't mean we don't love you or—"

"Don't give me that crap!" Lauren shouted, cutting Shawn off. "That's what people say to babies. I'm not a *baby!* Tell me the truth. Tell me why you're *doing* this! I know it's not Daddy. He wouldn't do this. He wouldn't leave us!"

Shawn's shoulders sagged. "Sweetheart, I…I'm so sorry. But this was a mutual decision. And it doesn't mean Dad's leaving *you.* It just means…it's impossible for us to stay married." If only she could tell Lauren the truth. Make her see that staying married to Rick was not an option. But Lauren adored her father. And Shawn didn't want to crush *all* of Lauren's illusions by telling her he'd been having an affair with his young assistant. The same young assistant Shawn had taken under her wing. The same young assistant who had cried on Shawn's shoulder when her father had died the previous year. The same young assistant Shawn had begun to think of as another daughter. In some ways, Alexandra's betrayal was even worse than Rick's.

"I don't *believe* you," Lauren said. "I'll ask Daddy. *He'll* tell me the truth. You *must* know where he is! He…he wouldn't just *leave!*"

"Honey, I *don't* know where he is. But he said he'd call. I—I'm assuming he's staying in a hotel." What Shawn really thought was that Rick had hotfooted it right over to Alexandra's condo, but that was one more thing she couldn't tell Lauren.

Lauren's face twisted. "I'll never forgive you for this. Never. You're ruining my life!" And with that, she swung around and raced out of the room, down the hall and up the stairs.

Shawn flinched when she heard Lauren's door slam. Trembling, Shawn sank down onto the chair Lauren had vacated. She stared unseeingly into the distance. She shuddered in remembrance of the bleak look in Lauren's eyes as she'd shouted that she would never forgive Shawn.

This is all your fault, Rick. All your fault. You don't deserve to keep your daughter's good opinion. And I certainly don't deserve to have her blame me for wrecking our family….

A flood of emotion swamped Shawn, and she could feel tears trying to erupt again, but she fought them off. She'd cried herself to sleep last night and that was enough. She promised herself she would not waste another ounce of emotional energy on her faithless husband and his equally faithless assistant.

From now on, she and Lauren were the only ones who mattered, the *only* ones.

And Rick and Alexandra could go straight to hell.

Chapter One

Six weeks later

"I saw a lawyer today."

"Shawn! Good for you. I was afraid you might be having second thoughts." The speaker was Ann O'Brien, one of the Wednesday Night Gang, a group of friends with whom Shawn had been having Wednesday dinners for the past several years. The women always met at Callie's Corner Café, which was located on the village square in what passed for Maple Hills' downtown.

Shawn grimaced. "No. I'm definitely going ahead

with the divorce. In fact, my lawyer was going to file the papers today. It's just that coping with the sale of my parents' house and trying to decide what to do with their belongings…" Even this brief reference to her parents caused her voice to break, and it took a moment to compose herself and continue. "Not to mention the problems with Lauren…hasn't left much energy for dealing with Rick…*or* Alexandra…so I put off taking action until now."

"Is that stupid girl still trying to patch things *up* with you?" Ann asked in disbelief.

Shawn nodded tiredly. "She called again this week. I thought it was Rick calling, so I had to pick up the phone. I immediately hung up when I realized it was her. I have nothing to say to her, and I don't have any interest in listening to what she has to say, either."

"The girl is totally clueless! If you're considering violence, count me in."

Everyone laughed, even Shawn. The wisecrack had come from Zoe Madison who, at thirty-nine, was the oldest member of their group. But not by much, Shawn thought. She would be there herself in a couple of months. And then forty… Fear snaked through her.

Forty and divorced.

Shawn had never imagined her life would turn out like this. When she'd married Rick, she'd envisioned them with three or four children, growing old together, welcoming grandchildren and, if they were lucky, great grandchildren. She'd dreamed of a golden wedding-anniversary party with all their family gathered round to celebrate with them. She swallowed. Now what? Would she be alone for the rest of her life?

"Hey, you okay?" Ann asked softly.

Shawn shook away her depressing thoughts. "I'm fine."

"Is Lauren still blaming you?" Carol Carbone, Ann's younger sister, gave Shawn a sympathetic look.

Shawn listlessly poked at her salad. "I'm afraid so." She sighed. "I'm still wondering if I did the right thing in not telling her why I want this divorce."

"Personally, I think you were too damned easy on Rick," Ann said. "I'd've kicked his sorry butt out the door when I first found those ticket stubs *and* I wouldn't have had any qualms about telling Lauren."

"I don't agree."

All five women looked at Emma Madison who, at not quite twenty-two, was the youngest member of their group.

"A girl needs to feel her father is a hero," Emma said. She avoided her mother's eyes.

For a moment, there was an awkward silence. They all knew Zoe had gotten pregnant with Emma when she was only seventeen and had never told Emma who her father was. As far as Shawn knew, Zoe had never told anyone.

"I think you did the right thing, too," Susan Pickering, the sixth and final member of the group, said, reaching over and squeezing Shawn's hand. "You took the high road, and some day, when Lauren's older, she'll understand how much you care about her."

Shawn smiled sadly. "Thanks." She hoped Susan was right.

"Which lawyer did you pick?" Zoe asked.

"Stella Vogel."

"Oh, you *did* call her!" Carol said.

Shawn nodded. "I did. I figured if your boss recommended her, she must be good."

Carol speared a shrimp. "John says she's the best."

"Does Lauren know?" Zoe asked.

Shawn shook her head. "Not yet." Then she made a face. "One thing at a time, you know?"

The women all murmured sympathetically. They knew Shawn had gotten a call from Lauren's English teacher, who was concerned because Lauren, who had always been an exceptional student, was falling behind in her schoolwork.

"What did Lauren say when you asked her about school?" Carol said.

Shawn shook her head. "She told me not to worry about it. That's her answer for everything nowadays. Then she said, *Don't pretend you care about me. We both know better, don't we?*"

"Oh, Shawn," Carol said.

Shawn wished she could wipe the memory of Lauren's hateful look and hurtful words out of her mind, but they were branded there.

"She doesn't really mean that," Susan said, "she's just trying to punish you."

Shawn nodded. On one level, she understood that was exactly what Lauren was doing. On another, she wondered if she would ever again have a loving, close relationship with her daughter.

Ann reached over and patted Shawn's hand. "Chin up, girl. This, too, shall pass."

"Yes, I know." And Shawn *did* know things would improve. She grimaced. They had to. After all, as things now stood, there was nowhere to go but up.

Just then Callie Hudson, the owner of the café, walked over to their table. "How're you girls doing? Need anything? Fill-ups on iced tea or coffee?" Her dark eyes were warm and friendly.

Shawn smiled and shook her head. She liked Callie. They all did. A widow, she had bought the café from the previous owner about six years earlier, using the insurance money she'd gotten upon her husband's death. Together with her twenty-three-year-old daughter, Kristie, she'd built it into the most popular gathering place in town.

Everyone said they were fine, and Callie left. Once she was gone, Susan turned to Shawn. "So what did your lawyer have to say?"

"She gave me a list of information she needs—stuff

like bank accounts, savings and investments, information about Rick's retirement fund, IRAs, things like that. She also wanted to know about our health insurance coverage. Oh, and about my parents' estate."

"Your parents' estate?" Zoe said, frowning.

"Yes. Unfortunately, whatever I end up with after the closing on their house *could* be considered marital property since I'm still married."

"Oh, no!" This came from Ann. "That sucks."

Shawn sighed. "I know. I'm hoping Rick won't try to claim any portion of the money. It's not like it's going to be a fortune. They weren't wealthy and the house, although paid for, didn't bring a great price because it needs a lot of work. It belonged to my grandparents on my father's side, so it's pretty old." She had hated having to sell the house, but there really wasn't any other choice. If her parents had had substantial savings, Shawn might have been able to keep the house, but her father had never made a lot of money. In fact, looking at just how little they *did* have saved, Shawn wondered how her father would ever have been able to retire.

"What about insurance?" Zoe asked.

"They just had modest policies—enough to pay off their bills and bury them. There's very little left." In fact, there hadn't even been enough to fix the most glaring problems with their house. Shawn still considered it a miracle the Realtor she'd used had been able to sell it so quickly.

"I don't see how Rick could have a right to any part of your parents' estate," Zoe said.

"I'm going to let Stella worry about that," Shawn said. "I've got enough to worry about right now. Speaking of—" She looked at her watch. "I'd better be going. I told Lauren she could go study math with her friend Allison as long as she was home by nine-thirty, and it's almost that now."

The women all said goodbye and wished her luck, and Shawn left. It was a fairly short drive to the beautiful old neighborhood where Shawn and Rick had purchased their dream home eight years earlier. A stately two-story redbrick with black shutters and a double walnut front door, it sat at the crest of a sloping lawn on a quiet, shady street.

Shawn loved the house and had been fighting off the depressing thought that after the divorce she and Lauren might have to move. She prayed not, because moving, although wrenching for Shawn, would be even worse for Lauren. It was too bad her parents had lived more than two hours away or she and Lauren could just have moved into *their* house and at least then Lauren would have been someplace familiar and loved, someplace that wouldn't have felt alien….

Stop it. Quit wasting energy on things that aren't possible….

The house was dark when Shawn pulled into the driveway. She looked at the clock on the dash and frowned. Lauren was late.

Shawn's stomach knotted. Lately Lauren defied her on every count. If Shawn said black, Lauren said white. It didn't matter what the subject, Lauren took whatever side Shawn didn't. It was exhausting…and painful. Sometimes Shawn despaired of ever having her sweet daughter back.

The smell hit Shawn as soon as she entered the house. "Oh, no! I don't believe this."

Trixie, their chocolate Lab, whimpered from the corner of the kitchen where she was cowering. She knew she'd done something wrong.

Shawn switched on the light. Sure enough, Trixie had done her business in the middle of the hooked rug Shawn kept by the door to the mudroom. Luckily, Shawn hadn't stepped in it.

"Dammit, Lauren!" she swore. Lauren had promised to walk Trixie before leaving for Allison's house. *Promised.*

"I *said* I'd do it," she'd retorted in that snotty tone she'd adopted ever since Shawn had told her about the divorce. "You don't have to keep *harping* on it."

Shawn had bitten back a sigh. "I'm not harping. I'm simply reminding you that it's your responsibility to walk Trixie in the afternoons."

Trixie had been a birthday gift to Lauren from Rick, one Shawn hadn't been in favor of. The dog was still too young to go more than a few hours without having to go out, and unfortunately their neighborhood was zoned against fencing, so they had no choice but to walk her often.

"The least she could have done was put you in your crate," Shawn muttered as she cleaned up the mess, then tossed the rug into the washing machine. "C'mon, Trixie, let's go out for a walk."

Thirty minutes later, all prepared to give Lauren a good talking-to, Shawn and Trixie returned from their walk to find Lauren *still* hadn't come home.

"That does it. She's grounded," Shawn muttered as she headed for the phone.

"I'm sorry, Shawn, but she's not here," Allison's mother said a few minutes later.

"What time did she leave?"

"Um, the thing is, Lauren hasn't been here at all tonight."

"What?"

"Allison had church group tonight. She got home about ten minutes ago."

Shawn closed her eyes. Dear God. What was she going to do with Lauren? And where on earth *was* she? With trembling fingers, she punched in the number for Rick's cell phone. He answered on the second ring.

"Is Lauren with you?" Shawn said without preamble.

"Hello, Shawn. Yes, she's here."

"Did you know she didn't tell me she was going to your place? Did you know she lied to me and said she was going to be at Allison's tonight, studying?"

"No, of course I didn't know that."

"How did she get there, anyway?" Rick lived a good six miles away on the other side of town.

"She came in a cab."

Shawn's mouth dropped open. "A cab!"

"She said it was too cold to ride her bike."

"And I suppose you said that was okay." Shawn sank down onto a kitchen chair. "Let me speak to her, Rick."

"Look," he said in a much lower voice, "she's kind of upset right now. Why don't you wait and talk to her tomorrow?"

"Tomorrow! Is she planning on spending the night, then?"

"She brought an overnight bag."

"What's she upset about now? Did something happen?" When he didn't immediately answer, she said, "Dammit, Rick! Will you answer me?"

"She said you told her she couldn't go to the spring dance."

"I did not tell her she couldn't go to the spring dance. I told her she couldn't go with Tiffany Underwood and her date." Tiffany Underwood was a senior Lauren had met through their karate lessons. Lauren was only a sophomore.

"I thought you liked Tiffany," Rick said.

"I do, but Lauren is too young to be double-dating with her. Especially since Tiffany's date is even older. He's twenty and goes to Ohio State. And he drives a

Hummer!" Once again Rick didn't answer right away. "You'd better back me up on this one, Rick. I mean it."

His sigh was audible. "Okay, sure."

"Well, don't you *agree?*"

"Yeah. I do. It's just that she's so unhappy right now, I hate to—"

"And whose fault is that?" Shawn said, interrupting him.

Another sigh. "C'mon, Shawn. Jeez. I made a mistake. Haven't *you* ever made a mistake?"

"Yes, I've made mistakes, but this was a bit more than a mistake, Rick, and you know it. The two of you had a full-blown affair going. For more than a year! She was going on business trips with you, and you lied, saying you'd given her time off while you were gone so I wouldn't get suspicious if I called your office. And all through the year, Alexandra was calling me and coming over here for dinner and holidays, just as if everything was the same. *That's* what I can't forgive. That the two of you—the husband I trusted and loved and the girl I had befriended and had begun to love—were betraying me over and over again."

"I told you how sorry I am. I know it was wrong. I— I just couldn't seem to help myself."

"That's bull and you know it. Tell me something, Rick. Have you stopped seeing Alexandra? Fired her? Told her to get lost?"

"Not yet, but I—"

"That's what I thought." After a moment, she added, "You know, Rick, I'm tired of always being the bad guy. I'm tired of Lauren running to you every time she gets upset with me. This isn't going to work. You're going to have to tell her the truth."

"The truth!"

"Yes, the truth."

"You can't mean that."

Shawn closed her eyes. Part of her wanted to shout at him, tell him she *did* mean it, and if he weren't such a coward, he'd have *already* told his daughter the truth. But the other part of her, the adult, mature, mother part of her, knew it would be wrong to destroy the last of Lauren's innocence. "Let's put it this way. If you want to preserve your image in your daughter's eyes, you'll stop allowing her to believe that you're the injured party and start helping her understand that this divorce is for the best and that you want it, too."

"But I *don't* want a divorce, Shawn. That's what I've been trying to tell you, but you won't listen. And I don't think it's for the best. Certainly it's not best for Lauren."

"Look, Rick, I'll say it one last time. I cannot live with a liar. What you did completely destroyed my trust…and the love I had for you. Neither one is something that will magically come back just because you now say you're sorry. You made the choice to betray your marriage vows, and now we all have to live with the consequences."

"Jesus, Shawn, you're hard—"

"If I am, it's because I have to be. It's a matter of survival." Running her free hand through her hair, Shawn made a quick decision. "Lauren can stay the night. But I want you to tell her she can't come to your place again unless she has my permission. Do you understand?"

"Shawn…"

"Do you understand?"

"All right. I'll tell her."

"And make sure you sound like you mean it. *Without* blaming me."

"Fine," he snapped.

"I'm dead serious, Rick. I am not going to be the bad guy anymore. And one last thing. Make sure you get her to school on time. The last time she stayed overnight at your place, she missed her first class. Don't let it happen again."

And with that, she broke the connection.

Lauren could hear her father talking to her mother. They were arguing, but what else was new? They never did anything else, anymore.

What was *wrong* with her mother? Why was she acting like this? Was it because Grandma and Grandpa had died? Lauren swallowed. She couldn't stand to think about her Gibson grandparents. She missed them so much. Grandma Margaret, especially. She'd been so neat, not like an old person at all. She'd been a dancer when she was young, had even been with the Rockettes in New York for two years before she'd married Grandpa. She'd had all her old costumes and her tap shoes in a big trunk up in the attic of her house, and when Lauren was little, she'd let her play dress-up with them.

She used to laugh and say she didn't know how someone who loved to dance as much as she had could have married a man with two left feet. But she'd always given Lauren's grandfather such a sweet look when she said it that Lauren knew it didn't matter that Grandpa couldn't dance. Grandma Margaret had loved him, anyway.

If only I could talk to Grandma...I'll bet she'd fix things....

Heather always teased Lauren about how she was always calling her grandmother. Heather had thought it was weird, but Lauren had loved talking to her grandmother.

Until lately, she'd liked talking to her mom, too. But not now. Not since she'd kicked her dad out of the house. She was being so mean to Lauren's dad. And he hadn't done anything to deserve it.

Lauren felt so bad for her dad. He didn't want a divorce. And she hadn't needed him to tell her so to know, either. All she had to do was look at him to see how sad he was, how much he wanted to come back home. The whole thing *sucked!*

How could her mother do this to them? What was

wrong with her? It was like she wanted to change her whole life.

She wasn't even seeing Alexandra anymore. Lauren guessed that was because Alexandra worked for Lauren's dad, but that didn't seem fair.

Lauren missed Alexandra. She was cool.

I'm going to call her.

Maybe Alexandra could help her figure out what was wrong with her mother and give her some idea of what to do to make things right.

Picking up her cell phone, she looked up Alexandra's number, then placed the call. After four rings, Alexandra's voice mail kicked in. *Hi, this is Alexandra. Leave a message. I'll call you back.*

"Oh, hi, Alexandra," Lauren said, disappointed. "Um, this is Lauren. I wanted to talk to you. Could you call me back? On my cell?" Just in case Alexandra had lost Lauren's cell-phone number, Lauren repeated it. She ended her message by saying, "I miss you."

Dispirited, she disconnected the call and stared into space. A few minutes later, she heard her dad in the hallway outside her door. A moment later, he knocked.

"C'mon in, Dad."

Lauren had always thought her dad was the handsomest grown man she'd ever met. He was tall—Lauren liked tall men—and he had thick dark hair and the bluest eyes. He reminded her of Pierce Brosnan, except her dad was younger. Tonight, though, he looked older than normal. That was because he was sad, she knew.

She smiled at him as he approached the bed, then sat on the end. "I heard you talking to Mom."

He nodded.

"She was mad, right?"

"Look, Lauren…" He seemed to be trying to figure out what to say. "She had a right to be mad. You know? I mean, you should have told her you were coming here."

Lauren shrugged. "Whatever."

"Lauren…" he said softly.

Lauren looked away.

"Your mother loves you, you know. She worries about you."

"Yeah, sure."

"From now on, I don't want you to come here unless you have her permission."

Lauren's head snapped up. "Permission? Why do I need permission to see my own father?"

"Look, honey, you can't just go off and do whatever you want to do without telling Mom."

"Fine. I'll leave her a note next time."

"Lauren, please. For my sake, will you just ask your mother if you can come here when you want to come? If she says no, then I'll talk to her. But she won't. All she wants is for you to treat her with respect."

"Like she treats *me?*" Lauren didn't want to cry, but

she couldn't help it. "I know you don't want this divorce, Daddy. I know it's *her*. I don't want to live with her anymore. I want to live with you. Please? Can I come here to live?"

"Honey, you know that won't work. I have to go out of town on business too much of the time, and you'd be all alone here. You belong with your mother."

No matter what Lauren said, she couldn't sway her father. He just kept saying it wouldn't work, but Lauren knew the reason he was saying no was that he didn't want to make her mother any madder at him than she already was.

I hate her. She's ruined everything.

When he finally left, Lauren turned out the lights and cried herself to sleep.

By the time Lauren came home the following afternoon, Shawn had calmed down. She'd reminded herself yet again that Lauren was suffering. She'd not only lost the grandparents she'd loved dearly, she'd also lost her feeling of safety and security at home, and the only way she could deal with her emotions was by lashing out at Shawn, both directly and indirectly. Still, Shawn would have to talk to her about neglecting Trixie as well as failing to ask permission to go to Rick's.

But when Lauren walked in, Shawn took one look at her daughter's red, puffy eyes—obviously, something had happened at school to upset her—and her heart wrenched with love and pity.

In the old days—BRB (before Rick's betrayal)—Shawn would have immediately asked Lauren what was wrong and they would have talked.

Now, however, she knew she had to tread softly. So all she said was "Hi, honey."

Lauren mumbled something that could have been "hi."

Shawn's arms itched to hold Lauren. To smooth back her hair and kiss her forehead the way she had when Lauren had been a little girl. But she'd been rebuffed so many times over the past weeks, she forced herself to continue taking items from the refrigerator in preparation for making meatloaf for their dinner. "If you're hungry, there are some of those—"

But Lauren was already gone, her feet racing up the stairs, her bedroom door slamming shut with a bang that caused Shawn to close her eyes and bow her head. Despite her best effort to keep her emotions in check, her eyes filled with tears. Immediately, she was angry with herself. Hadn't she cried enough in the past months? Taking a deep breath, she groped for a tissue, wiped her eyes, then blew her nose.

She could hear Lauren upstairs. Her room was directly over the kitchen. When the noise stopped, Shawn knew Lauren was probably lying across her bed talking on the phone. Walking over to the portable unit on the kitchen counter, Shawn picked it up. Yes, the line was in use.

Shawn's shoulders sagged with the realization that these days Lauren would rather talk to anyone else than her mother. Sometimes Shawn wasn't sure she could keep going. And yet, what choice did she have?

Chapter Two

Matt McFarland could hardly wait until the day was over. On afternoons like this, he wondered why he'd ever wanted to be a teacher, especially a high-school teacher.

All day he'd been watching the kids in his classes fidget and pass notes and pretend to be working, when it was obvious they were doing anything but. The trouble was the weather. It was too nice, one of those rare March days that fooled you into thinking spring had actually arrived, even though by the end of the week, they were supposed to have another cold front come down from Canada.

But that was days away. Today everyone wanted to be outdoors, even him.

As he looked over his classroom, his attention was caught by Lauren Fletcher, who sat staring out the window. It wasn't the first time he'd been struck by how unhappy she seemed, and he'd been trying to decide what, if anything, he could do about it, because whatever it was that was bothering her was affecting her work.

Lauren was one of three sophomore students who had been chosen to represent Maple Hills High School in the state math competition that would be held in Columbus in May. The students had been picked based on their math average at the end of their freshman year. But Lauren's performance so far this semester was anything but stellar. And if it kept up this way, there wouldn't be much point in sending her to State.

Matt knew he needed to talk to Lauren, try to get to the bottom of whatever it was that was troubling her, maybe see if he could help her. But if Matt was going to help Lauren, he'd have to do it in a way that wouldn't cause her to clam up. After giving the problem some thought over the past week, he'd decided to ask her to work with him to develop a study program she and the other participants could follow in preparation for the competition. Hopefully, this would be a first step toward gaining her confidence.

So when the bell rang signaling the end of the period, he called her over. Sitting on the edge of his desk, he said casually, "Lauren, it's time to start preparing for the competition. I was wondering if you'd like to help me put a study program together."

A pleased smile brightened her blue eyes. "Oh. Okay. Sure, I'd like to help."

"How about meeting here after school tomorrow?"

"I can't tomorrow. I have my karate lesson on Tuesdays."

"What about Thursday?"

"Thursday would work."

"Well, check with your parents and make sure it's okay, and if it is, we'll plan on Thursday."

"I don't need to check with my parents."

If what she'd said hadn't sounded alarm bells, the abrupt change in her expression would have told Matt that he might have just hit on the root of her problem. For a moment, he didn't answer. Then, quietly, he said, "Lauren, is something wrong?"

She shrugged, avoiding his gaze.

Matt knew the value of silence, so instead of pushing, he waited.

"They're getting a divorce," she finally said in a voice so low he had to strain to hear her.

When her eyes met his again, he saw tears shimmering there. He felt a rush of pity. Poor kid. Divorce was tough on everyone, especially the kids.

"I'm sorry," Matt said.

Lauren swallowed, then nodded. "Thanks."

"Listen, Lauren, maybe you should think about talking to Mrs. Adler." Connie Adler was the school counselor and, as far as Matt could tell from his short time in Maple Hills, a sensible woman who seemed to have a knack for dealing with teenage angst, even though she was overwhelmed with the administrative duties continually heaped upon her.

"Why? Talking to her won't change anything."

Matt hated hearing that kind of bitterness in the voice of a fifteen-year-old. "It might help you deal with things, though."

"The only thing that'll help is if my dad can come home."

"Well, if you change your mind…"

"I won't."

Matt smothered a sigh. At least he'd found out what the problem was. That was a start. And now that she'd opened up once, she might again. The kid obviously needed someone she could talk to.

After she'd gone, Matt cleaned up his desk, put the two pop quizzes he'd given his geometry and algebra classes into his satchel to grade tonight, then headed out to the faculty parking lot. Climbing into his Jeep Wrangler, he thought about hitting the gym but decided he'd rather just put on his running clothes and get his exercise outdoors today. Might as well take advantage of the nice weather while they had it.

As he drove toward the small house he was renting with an option to buy, Matt thought he might just like to settle here permanently. It was too soon to tell; after all, he'd only been in Maple Hills since January, but he really liked the town.

A native of Cleveland, Matt had spent the past eight years since acquiring his master's degree teaching math in the Cleveland school system. But after a painful breakup of a relationship he'd believed would end in marriage, he'd decided he needed a complete change of scenery. When his sister Cathy had told him about the opening at the high school for a math teacher, Matt had decided to look into it. The school and its principal had impressed Matt. Taking the job had been a no-brainer. So far, Matt wasn't sorry he'd made the move. The town was everything Cathy had touted it to be: picturesque, friendly, progressive and a good place to live.

It was also a definite plus that Cathy and her husband and two children had moved to Maple Hills a year earlier. At forty-three, she was eleven years older than Matt, but theirs was a close family, so the age difference didn't matter. Cathy had taught kindergarten for years, first in the Cleveland area, then in Columbus where her husband, Lowell, a big-shot executive, worked for a large insurance company, and now in Maple Hills. Lowell still worked for the same company, and said the forty-five-minute drive into the city was worth it considering his kids now had the opportunity to live in a small town.

The only fly in the ointment seemed to be Cathy's

determination to find a girl for Matt. No matter how many times Matt told her he preferred getting his own dates, she continued to try to fix him up with one female acquaintance after another.

In fact, she'd wanted Matt to come to a dinner party Saturday night, but Matt had begged off, knowing there would be an extra female there earmarked for him.

Instead, Matt had spent Saturday night painting the kitchen cabinets, which sorely needed it, while keeping one eye on the Cavaliers' game.

Pulling into the driveway of his house, he couldn't help feeling a sense of satisfaction. He'd pretty much made up his mind to buy the house. It wasn't new and it needed lots of work, but it had charm. A fifties-style bungalow, it had a screened-in back porch, a large yard and a wealth of trees. This was the first time since Matt had joined the working world that he'd lived anywhere but an apartment, and he found he liked it. He was even thinking of getting a dog, a luxury he'd never even considered in his apartment days.

Entering the house, he noted that the paint smell was almost gone. It'd soon be back, though. He planned to paint the living room over the coming weekend. Tossing his satchel on the kitchen table, he headed for the bedroom and a change of clothes.

Fifteen minutes later, dressed to run, he set off down the street. Several of his neighbors waved to him as he jogged by and he waved back. He thought what a friendly town this was as he turned the corner and headed toward the city park.

Others had had the same idea about the nice weather, he saw when he got there ten minutes later, for the trail had quite a few runners.

He quickly settled into a comfortable rhythm behind a group of three women. Although normally he would have passed them after a few minutes, today he wasn't in any hurry to be anywhere else, so he decided to just enjoy the view. All three of the women had good bodies, but the one in the middle—a curly-haired blonde— was particularly nice to look at, with slender legs and the best-looking butt Matt had seen in a long time. He was concentrating so hard on watching it that he didn't see the rock sticking up in the middle of his side of the trail and couldn't catch his balance when his right toe struck it, pitching him forward.

He hit the ground hard, scraping his knees and arms but managing to keep his face protected. The three women stopped and turned around to see what had happened, and the older man running behind him also stopped.

"You okay?" the man said, reaching down to help Matt up.

"Yeah, I'm fine," Matt said, brushing himself off, but he could see his right knee was bleeding. "Damn," he muttered, feeling like a fool. His left ankle hurt, too. He'd twisted it.

The women all murmured concern, and the one whose backside Matt had so admired reached into the pocket of her shorts and pulled out a handful of Band-Aids. "Here," she said, "have one."

"You carry *Band-Aids* when you run?" one of the other women—the tallest one—asked incredulously.

The blonde, who had incredible green eyes, smiled sheepishly. "I like to be prepared."

"Shawn, you constantly amaze me," said the third woman, an attractive redhead.

"Thanks," Matt said to the blonde. Shawn, he thought. He liked her name. Fumbling with the paper wrap on the bandage, he dropped the first one.

"Here, let me help you," she said. "Zoe, have you got any tissues?"

The redhead dug in the pocket of her fleece jacket and produced a couple of crumpled ones.

By now the older man, apparently deciding the women would tend to Matt and he wouldn't be needed, had taken off after saying Matt should probably go get his scrapes taken care of.

The blonde—jeez, Matt wished he'd met her under other, more flattering, circumstances—dabbed at his knee, then competently tore the paper wrapping off another of the bandages and placed it on the cut. "There. You need to clean that thoroughly, then put some kind of antibiotic ointment on it after you do, okay?"

The redhead rolled her eyes. "Always the mother."

"Thanks," Matt said. He couldn't help but notice the blonde wasn't wearing a wedding band.

"Shawn, c'mon," the third woman said. "I've gotta get home by five."

Before Matt—who was going to introduce himself—could say anything else, the blonde gave him a sorry-gotta-go kind of smile and the three women took off. Matt stood uncertainly, and by the time he'd decided to go after them and find out the blonde's last name, they were too far ahead for him to catch up, especially since his right knee was throbbing and his left ankle ached.

Oh, hell, he thought. Opportunity had knocked, and he hadn't opened the door fast enough. Turning around, he limped toward the entrance and home and put the blonde and her enticing backside out of his mind.

"He was cute, wasn't he?" Carol said.

Shawn smiled. "He was." Poor guy. She'd felt sorry for him. She could see how embarrassed he'd been over his fall. "Too young for us, though."

"Think so?" Carol said.

"I know so." He couldn't have been a day over twenty-seven or -eight, Shawn thought, once more remembering that looming fortieth birthday of hers.

"They say younger men are great in bed," Zoe said dryly.

"Zoe, do you ever think about anything other than sex?" Carol said.

"If I ever *got* any, I wouldn't have to think about it," Zoe muttered.

Shawn and Carol laughed, but underlying their amusement was the all-too-realistic awareness that none of them were getting any younger and unless they wanted to have one-night stands—which they didn't—sex might just be a thing of the past.

It wasn't for Alexandra and Rick, though, Shawn thought bitterly. They were probably doing it morning, noon and night. *Forget about them. They aren't worth two seconds of your time.*

But for the remainder of her run, she couldn't seem to banish them from her thoughts. By the time she had said goodbye to Carol and Zoe and climbed into her little Honda SUV for the drive home, Shawn had once more replayed the scene where she'd caught them having sex. And not just having sex. Having sex in *her* house.

It was such a cliché. The wife goes out of town to finish packing up her parents' belongings but decides to come home a day earlier than she'd planned.

And finds a surprise.

Shawn still couldn't believe Rick had been so careless, so thoughtless. Yes, Shawn had been away, but Lauren had been in town, spending the night at a friend's house. What if *she* had unexpectedly come home? And had found her father and the young woman she admired and looked up to having sex on the living-room floor the way her mother had?

Suddenly, all Shawn wanted was for her divorce decree to come quickly. Maybe once her marriage was legally dead, she could forget about the pain of Rick's betrayal, move on and start to build a new life.

Lauren stood at her locker, oblivious to the other kids milling around. She wished she could skip this last period, but she was going to meet with Mr. McFarland again this afternoon, so she couldn't. He'd asked her earlier today if she would mind staying again tonight. She'd wanted to tell him that working with him last Thursday was the best part of her week, but of course, she didn't.

But it was true. He was so nice. So sweet, even. Not like a teacher at all, more like her friend. And he was so easy to talk to, probably because he really listened. Lauren had found herself telling him things she hadn't even told Heather, and Heather was her best friend. Things like how she felt about her father and how much it hurt to go home and not see him there. When she'd told him about her mother and how *she* was the one who wanted the divorce—no matter *what* her father tried to pretend—Lauren could see that Mr. McFarland knew what she was feeling, and that he agreed with her that all this was her mother's fault.

She doesn't care about me anymore. Mothers are supposed to be unselfish. They're supposed to care about their kids.

Suddenly Lauren winced and clutched her stomach. The pain was bad today. She closed her eyes, willed it to go away. But it kept burning.

"Hey, Lauren, you okay?"

Lauren blinked. Swallowed. Heather, her face all worried, was standing there. "I—I'm fine."

"You sure?"

Lauren groped in her backpack for the package of antacids she'd been carrying around for weeks now. They seemed to help when the pain came. Furtively popping a couple in her mouth—they weren't allowed to carry any kind of drug in school—she chewed. "It's just heartburn. Prob'ly from that pizza we ate for lunch."

Heather rolled her eyes. "Yeah, I keep saying I'm not gonna buy it anymore. It's so greasy."

Lauren nodded. "Well, I'd better get going. I'm gonna be late for French."

The pain pretty much went away by the time her French class was over, and Lauren hurried to her locker to gather up what she wanted to take home that night, then headed toward the stairs. Mr. McFarland's classroom was on the second floor.

"Hey, Lauren, wait up!"

Lauren turned to see Heather hurrying toward her.

"Want to go to Burger Barn?" Heather said. "Me and Allison are going." She grinned. "I think Lance and Ryan will be there." Heather currently had a huge crush on Ryan Holmes, one of the stars of the Maple Hills High varsity basketball team.

"Can't. I'm working with Mr. McFarland again today."

Heather's grin got bigger. "Ooooo."

Lauren frowned. "What?"

"You know…"

"No, I don't. What are you talking about?"

"Mr. McFarland. He's hot, that's all."

Lauren could feel her face heating. *Damn.* She hated when she blushed. "Heather, he's a *teacher*."

"So? He's still hot." Her smile turned sly. "Don't tell me you didn't notice."

"No, I didn't notice." But she *had* noticed, and now she was afraid Heather knew it. "Listen," she said, flustered. "I've gotta go. I'll call you later, okay?" Before Heather could say anything else, Lauren rushed off. Two minutes later, she knocked on Mr. McFarland's closed door.

"C'mon in," he called.

She took a deep breath and told herself to calm down. He couldn't possibly know what she and Heather had been talking about. There was no reason to be nervous.

Lauren opened the door and walked in.

Shawn stared at Stella Vogel. "What do you mean, there's very little money? That's impossible."

Stella, a diminutive firecracker of a woman, gave Shawn a sympathetic look. "I'm sorry, Shawn. I hate being the bearer of bad news, but it looks like your husband has been cashing in investments over the past two years."

Shawn couldn't take it in. Last time she'd looked, they'd had more than forty thousand dollars in stocks as well as a hefty chunk in a CD. What had happened to the money? Had he been spending it on Alexandra?

Shawn sat there numbly, her heart pounding.

No money.

What was she going to do? Oh God. Now there was no way she could keep the house. It would be impossible. "Wh-what about his 401(k)?"

"The good news is, he can't touch the 401(k) unless he leaves the company or retires. The bad news is, he's borrowed money against it."

Shawn just sat there. She couldn't seem to move. Or even to think.

"Shawn," Stella said matter-of-factly, "I know this is a blow, but I think we can get the house for you."

Shawn swallowed. "But without any money, I won't be able to afford to keep it. It…it's expensive to maintain. And there's a big mortgage." Thank God for the money from the sale of her parents' home, but she'd need that money as a safety net. She couldn't afford to sink it all into the house. She looked away. Stared out Stella's office window. "I haven't worked at a paying job since Lauren was born. I don't even know if I have any skills that are marketable anymore."

"You're a smart woman, and all that volunteer work you've done over the past years has given you skills you probably don't even realize you have."

Shawn knew the attorney was trying to make her feel better, and she appreciated the woman's sympathy and understanding, but Shawn knew volunteer work wasn't going to impress potential employers the way a history of paying positions would.

By the time Shawn left Stella's office, she was no longer shocked over the money situation. Instead she was furious, and not just with Rick. She was also furious with herself. Why had she allowed Rick to handle all their financial affairs? Why hadn't she made sure she was involved and aware of what was going on with their money?

She'd been a blind, trusting fool living in a fool's paradise. Angry tears burned her eyes as she remembered how she'd believed that since Rick earned all the money, it was only right he make the decisions concerning their finances. When Zoe had told her it wasn't smart to be out of the loop, Shawn had gotten irritated at Zoe's implied criticism of Rick and had even told her so.

God! How *could* she have been so stupid?

You know how. You liked not having to think about finances. You liked that Rick earned a lot of money and you had the nicest home of all your friends and didn't have to work for a salary. You liked the fact you could be Lady Bountiful and spend your time doing charity work. You felt sorry for Carol—who complained about her job all the time and who you knew envied you and your cushy life—and Zoe, who'd always had to work so hard and had never had the opportunity to travel the way you did.

Well, now you're paying the price for all those years of enjoying life. Now you've been pushed into the real world.

And somehow you'll have to figure out how to live in it.

Matt sat at his desk for a long time after Lauren Fletcher had left. He kept seeing the look of pain on her face—and this time the pain hadn't been solely emotional.

He'd finally gotten her to admit that she'd been having sharp, burning pains in her stomach for the past few weeks, and that she'd been popping antacids to keep it controlled. Another teacher might have reported her for the use of forbidden drugs, but Matt had no intention of doing so.

"It's just heartburn," she'd said, "no big deal."

But heartburn pain occurred in the chest. That's why it was called heartburn. What Lauren was experiencing sounded an awful lot like the beginnings of an ulcer, and with what the kid had been going through lately, it wouldn't surprise Matt at all if that turned out to be the case. And ulcers were nothing to fool around with. Lauren needed to see a doctor. She needed to be on the appropriate medication. She needed less stress in her life.

What the hell was wrong with her mother that she couldn't see what bad shape Lauren was in? Was she as self-centered as Lauren claimed? Matt knew how dramatic teenagers could be, especially teenage girls, so he had taken what Lauren had said about her mother with a grain of salt. Now, though, he wondered. Maybe the woman really *didn't* care about Lauren, or maybe she was so shell-shocked over the divorce, she was oblivious.

Damn. Although he didn't want to, Matt knew he was going to have to get involved. After packing up his gear and locking his desk, he headed for the office.

Five minutes later, armed with the Fletchers' home phone number, Matt headed home. That night, hoping Lauren wouldn't be the one to answer the phone, he placed the call he'd decided to make.

"Hello?"

The voice at the other end was softer than Matt had been prepared for and, for a moment, he was taken aback. "Mrs. Fletcher?"

"Yes?"

"Mrs. Fletcher, this is Matt McFarland. I'm Lauren's math teacher."

"Oh?" Now her voice sounded wary.

"I don't know if Lauren mentioned it, but she's been

helping me develop a study program for her and the other students who will be participating at State this year."

"I see. No, she didn't mention it."

"Look, I'll come right to the point. I'm worried about Lauren, and I'd like to talk to you. Could you possibly come by after school tomorrow?"

"I, um, yes, I can do that. What time?"

"How about four-thirty? The kids are all usually cleared out by then."

"All right. Where will you be?"

Matt told her how to find his classroom, then said, "Are you going to tell Lauren I called?"

"No, I don't think so."

"Good. It would probably upset her."

It would do more than upset her, he thought as they said goodbye. She would feel betrayed. Matt knew he was doing the right thing. He only hoped Lauren would eventually see it that way, too.

Chapter Three

Shawn arrived at the school a few minutes before four-thirty. She was apprehensive about meeting with Lauren's math teacher. She knew he wouldn't have asked for a meeting if things were going well. Obviously, there was a problem, and it would be laid at her doorstep.

She realized it was an exercise in frustration, but she kept second-guessing herself, wondering if there was anything she could do differently that would make it easier for Lauren to cope with all the changes in her life.

You could tell her the truth, since Rick seems incapable of doing so.

Shawn gritted her teeth in frustration. Why couldn't

she tell Lauren? Why was it okay for their daughter to think badly of *her* but not of Rick?

You know why. Aside from the fact she'd probably shoot the messenger, the worst thing you could do is expose Rick for the cheater he is. When and if Lauren finds out the truth, it has to come from someone other than you. So stop feeling sorry for yourself. Just be the best mother you can be, and things will work out.

But *would* they? It was two and a half months since she'd told Lauren about the divorce, and if anything, Lauren seemed to be drifting even farther away.

I'm so tired of being strong. Oh, Mom, how I wish you were here. How I wish I could pick up the phone and tell you my troubles and have you tell me, the way you did when I was a little girl and cried on your shoulder, that everything would be okay.

But her mother was gone. Shawn was the grown-up now. Wearily, she parked her car in the visitor's lot, then walked to the main entrance. She still felt strange about the fact that every person entering the high school had to pass through a security check, including a metal detector, but she knew the safety measures that had been adopted a few years ago were, unfortunately, necessary.

After passing her through, the security guard pointed her toward the stairs, and Shawn went up to the second floor. Mr. McFarland's classroom was at the far end of the hall and she approached it slowly.

His door was closed. Shawn stood outside for a moment and gathered her thoughts. The last thing she wanted to do was go in there and be defensive. What she wanted was to have a constructive conversation and hear whatever suggestions the math teacher might have for helping Lauren through this difficult time.

Telling herself not to be nervous, she knocked, and a moment later the door opened.

Shawn stared, dumbfounded.

The good-looking young man standing there was none other than the runner who had fallen last week, the one who had taken the Band-Aid she'd offered, the one they'd thought was so cute. And he looked just as startled to see her.

"Mr. McFarland?"

"Yes." He frowned.

"I'm Shawn Fletcher. Lauren's mother."

"You're kidding. You don't look old enough to be Lauren's mother."

She laughed. "Oh, I'm old enough, all right."

He stood back. "C'mon in."

"Thank you." The tension she'd felt just a few minutes earlier eased. This was going to be fine. This man wasn't going to make her feel like a bad mother.

Once they were seated inside the classroom—him behind his desk but turned sideways so it wasn't between them, and her in a chair he'd pulled up to the side of the desk—he said, "Life is funny, isn't it? I didn't think I'd ever see you again."

She smiled. "Is your knee okay?"

"Yeah, it was just a scrape."

"That's good."

For a moment, they fell silent. Then he said, "Thank you for coming today."

"No. Thank *you*. I'm glad you called. I've been worried about Lauren for weeks."

"Me, too."

Shawn hesitated, then decided nothing would be gained by beating around the bush. "Did she tell you her father and I are in the process of getting a divorce?"

"Yes, she did."

"She's very upset about it."

"I know."

"She's talked to you about her feelings?" Shawn couldn't help feeling a pang at the thought that her daughter could confide in this man she'd only known since January. "She won't talk to me at all. She…" Shawn took a deep breath. "She blames me."

"I know."

"Mr. McFarland, please tell me what she said. I need to know."

"Okay, but before I do, I have a request of you."

"Anything."

"The name is Matt. Mr. McFarland is my father."

Shawn smiled. "Okay. I'll call you Matt, but only if you'll call me Shawn."

He smiled, too. "Deal." Then he sobered. "All right.

Lauren says she can't talk to you, that you don't listen to her."

"That's not true. The problem is I don't give her the answers she wants. What she wants is for her father and me to get back together, and that's not going to happen."

His dark eyes studied her thoughtfully. "Are you sure it won't?"

"Without a doubt. The divorce proceedings are well under way. All that's left is settling finances."

He nodded. "This is a tough time for both of you then."

"You have no idea how tough." Shawn swallowed. "My parents—Lauren's grandparents—were killed in an automobile accident in October. Did she tell you that, too?"

He shook his head slowly. "No. That's really rough. I'm sorry."

Shawn nodded. "Thank you." Her eyes met his. "And it's going to get rougher." She hadn't intended to tell him this but found herself saying, "I just found out that we will probably have to move."

He grimaced.

"I know," she said. "I'd hoped we could stay in the house and avoid another big change in Lauren's life, but it's not going to be financially feasible, I'm afraid."

"That's too bad."

"Yes." Shawn dreaded telling Lauren, yet she knew she couldn't put it off. She needed to get the house on the market as soon as possible, since it might take months to sell it, months when Shawn would be spending money she couldn't afford to spend. She made a mental note to call Ann tonight. Ann was a real estate agent.

"Did you know Lauren has been having bad stomach pains for a couple of weeks now?"

Shawn stared at Matt. "Ohmigod! What kind of pain? When did she tell you *this?*"

"She didn't tell me. I saw the look on her face yesterday when the pain hit. She said it was heartburn and took some antacids—something she's really not allowed to do on school grounds—but if I were you, I'd get her to a doctor."

Shawn wanted to cry. Poor Lauren. Her poor baby. "I can't believe she's been going through this and hasn't told me. I'll make sure she sees someone about it, whether she wants to or not."

"Good." His dark eyes were full of sympathy.

Sometimes Shawn felt so impotent. Her world had spiraled out of control, and she didn't have a clue how to get it on the right track again. "I know Lauren needs counseling," she said wearily, "but I can't even introduce the subject without her getting upset."

"Would you like me to talk to her about it?"

"Would you?"

"I already tried once—to get her to see the school counselor—but she said there was nothing Mrs. Adler could do to help." He smiled reassuringly. "But I'll try again. Maybe this time she'll be ready to hear it."

"I hope so, because it's obvious she needs more than either her dad or I are capable of giving her." Shawn's mind was working frantically. She would also talk to their doctor when she made an appointment for Lauren to see him. He could talk to Lauren about counseling, as well.

"Have you talked to her father about her problems?"

"Yes."

"Will he also urge her to see a therapist? I know what he says and thinks is important to her." Then he added, "I hope you don't think I'm butting in where I don't belong."

"No, of course I don't. I appreciate your concern. And you're right. I'll definitely talk to him about reinforcing the idea of counseling."

"Good." He smiled, leaning back in his chair. "You know, you're nothing like I thought you'd be."

Shawn's own smile was wry. "You probably thought I'd have two heads and be riding a broomstick."

Now he laughed. "Nothing that bad."

"C'mon, tell the truth. I'm sure Lauren painted me with a black brush. I know she thinks all of this is my fault. That I drove her father away."

"She needs someone to blame."

"And I'm an easy target."

He nodded.

He had the nicest eyes, Shawn decided. They were a warm, dark brown flecked with gold. Friendly eyes.

"The good news is," he said, "that Lauren's math grades have improved considerably from what they were at the start of the semester. And she's working hard to prepare for the math competition in Columbus."

"I think we have you to thank for that."

"You're giving me too much credit. She's the one doing the work."

"Well, whatever the reason, I'm just grateful she's doing better in school."

They continued to talk about Lauren's progress in math, then he said, "I'll talk to Mrs. Adler and see if she has any recommendations for a family therapist, then give you a call."

"Thank you. I'll ask our doctor, too. Oh, and would you call me on my cell phone instead of our home phone? I wouldn't want Lauren to get wind of this until we have a chance to talk to her about it." Shawn dug in her purse and pulled out a small notebook. Flipping it open, she wrote down her cellphone number and her e-mail address. Handing the information to him, she said, "You can always e-mail me, as well."

He reached into the center drawer of his desk and pulled out a business card. "This has got my cell-phone number and e-mail address on it. Don't hesitate to call or write if you have any questions or concerns."

"Thank you." Shawn put the card in her purse and rose. "I really appreciate this, Mr., um, Matt."

"Glad I could help. Like I said, I hadn't expected to see you again, so this was a pleasant surprise."

Although the last thing on Shawn's mind was another relationship—not to mention the fact Matt McFarland was way too young for her—she couldn't help thinking how nice it would be to meet someone like him eight or ten months from now when she might be ready to think about dating again. "For me, too," she said.

Driving home, Shawn replayed their conversation. She thought she knew why Lauren had felt so free to confide in him. It was because Matt inspired trust. And even though he had repeated some of the things Lauren had told him, he hadn't broken that trust. He had done what he was supposed to do—he had put the welfare of his student above any personal qualms he might have felt.

Shawn felt lighter just knowing she wasn't alone in her concern over Lauren.

Matt McFarland was a good guy, and he was on her side.

After Shawn left, Matt sat at his desk for a long time, thinking about their meeting. He couldn't get over who Lauren's mother had turned out to be and that she was so different from what he'd imagined. He also couldn't help liking and sympathizing with her.

Not only was she much younger than he'd imagined—he guessed she was close to his age, maybe thirty-five, tops—but she was soft spoken, warm and obviously very worried about Lauren. It didn't take a genius to see that Shawn loved Lauren very much and that she wanted nothing more than to make everything okay for the teenager.

Jeez, she'd had a rough time. First she'd lost her parents and now the divorce...

Matt wondered what was behind the divorce. He'd wanted to ask her, but of course, he couldn't. It was obvious Lauren didn't have a clue. She'd insisted several times that her parents had never fought, that they'd just suddenly announced they were splitting up, and that neither one of them would tell her anything.

Matt wondered if there was another woman. If that was the case, Lauren's father was stupid. Matt couldn't imagine any guy finding a woman more appealing than Shawn Fletcher. It wasn't just that she was beautiful and sexy—even though she was—but she was obviously intelligent and interesting and had a sense of humor.

Matt would date her in a heartbeat.

He wondered what she'd thought of *him*.

Now if his sister Cathy had introduced him to someone like Shawn, Matt wouldn't be so quick to deride blind dates.

His thoughts were still on Shawn when he got home later that afternoon. He had already decided he was going to do everything in his power to help her.

And who knew?

Maybe, in a few months, after her divorce was final, she would be ready to date again.

Matt would be first in line.

When a week had gone by and Lauren still hadn't heard from Alexandra, she decided to call her again. This time Alexandra answered the phone.

"Alexandra!" Lauren said, smiling. "I'm so glad you're home." When Alexandra didn't say anything, Lauren added, "It's Lauren."

"Yes, I know. Hi, Lauren."

Lauren frowned. Alexandra didn't sound very happy to hear from her. "Um, hi. Did you get my message? The one I left last week?"

"Yes, I did, and I'm sorry I didn't call you back, but I've been really busy."

"Oh."

"And actually, I'm getting ready to go somewhere right now, so I only have a minute."

"Oh."

"So…what did you want?"

"I—I just…I miss talking to you," Lauren blurted.

For a moment, Alexandra didn't answer. Then her voice softened. "I miss you, too."

"Then why don't you ever come over? I mean, just because my mom and dad are splitting up doesn't mean we can't be friends anymore, does it?"

"Lauren, I…it's not…have you talked to your mother about this?"

Lauren shook her head. "No. I—I can't."

"Why not?"

"Because we're not really talking to each other. I was hoping you could tell me what's going on. I know my dad probably tells you things. Do…do you know why they're getting a divorce?"

Once again it took Alexandra a long time to answer. "That's something else you need to talk to your parents about."

"But *do* you know why?"

"Lauren, please don't ask me these questions. I can't talk to you about this."

"No one will tell me anything!"

"Look, I'm sorry. I really am. But I really do have to go. I have an eight o'clock appointment, and if I don't leave in the next five minutes, I'll be late. You take care, okay? And talk to your dad if you can't talk to your mom. Tell him you talked to me, and I said he should explain things to you."

"Okay," Lauren whispered.

But her dad wouldn't tell her anything, either. He just kept saying the marriage between him and her mom hadn't worked out. Duh. She knew that. What she didn't know was *why*.

"You shouldn't have called Alexandra," he said.

"But why *not?*"

"Because this is between your mother and me. It doesn't concern anyone else."

Lauren blinked back tears. "It concerns me, too."

Her dad closed his eyes. Then he sighed. "I know it does, sweetheart. I'm sorry."

"Then why won't you *talk* to me?" Now Lauren was crying in earnest.

He put his arms around her and held her and patted her head. "Give me some time, okay? I promise that one day soon, I'll explain everything."

Lauren fumbled for a tissue and blew her nose. "You promise?"

He nodded. "I do."

Lauren guessed she'd have to be satisfied with that.

"Now I want you to promise *me* something."

"O-okay."

"I want you to see a therapist."

Lauren swallowed. "Mom talked to you, didn't she?" Her mother had brought up the subject of a family therapist the previous evening. And today, in school, Mr. McFarland had mentioned it again, too. Lauren couldn't help wondering if there was some kind of conspiracy going on.

"Yes, your mother called me this morning."

"I wish she'd just leave me alone." But Lauren didn't really wish that. What she wished was something completely different. Something hopeless. "First she wants me to go to the doctor because she thinks I have an ulcer, and then she wants me to see a shrink because she thinks I'm crazy."

"Neither one of us are going to leave you alone, Lauren. And neither one of us thinks you're crazy. It'll help you to talk to a professional. Someone who's objective."

"A shrink," she said stubbornly.

"A family therapist. Someone experienced in family problems. Someone who can help you deal with this."

She shrugged. "Fine. I'll go. But only because *you* want me to."

Her dad smiled slowly. "Good. When you go home tonight, tell your mother we talked and that she should make you an appointment."

Lauren wasn't convinced it would do her any good at all to talk to the shrink—her dad could fancy up his name, but Lauren knew better. Still, she'd promised, so she'd go.

So that night, when she got home, she told her mother she'd decided she would go to see a therapist if that's what she and her dad wanted.

"Oh, Lauren, sweetheart, I'm so glad."

It made Lauren feel kind of bad to see the sad look in her mother's eyes, but it also made her mad. *You don't have to be sad,* she wanted to shout. *Take Daddy back and we can all be a family again and then I won't need a shrink!*

The next day when Lauren got home from school, her mother said, "I've made an appointment for you with a therapist named Dr. Pennington. LeeAnn Pennington."

"A *woman?*"

"Yes. Is that okay?"

"Yeah. That's good." Lauren was pleased. It would be easier talking to a woman than to a man.

Of course, that wasn't true with Matt. *He* was easy to talk to. Although she'd been thinking of him as Matt for a while now, she was careful to address him as Mr. McFarland when she was with him and to refer to him that way when she talked about him to other people. She was even careful around Heather, never admitting that she had a huge crush on him.

He liked her, too. In fact, she could see him asking her out after she graduated. After all, there wasn't *that* much difference in their ages. Lauren would be sixteen soon—well, maybe not till September—but that wasn't *that* far off, and he was probably, what? Thirty? Maybe even only twenty-nine or twenty-eight. There might be as little as twelve years difference in their ages. Twelve years was only a big deal when you were a little kid. But once you became an adult, it was nothing.

"So when's the appointment?" she said now.

"Tomorrow after school."

Lauren frowned. "I'm supposed to be working on the math competition tomorrow."

"Yes, I know, but I called your math teacher and he said he'd change the session to Thursday."

"You called Ma...*Mr. McFarland?*" Crap! She'd almost said *Matt*. Glaring at her mother, she said, "Why did *you* call him? Why didn't you let *me* ask him? I wish you'd quit interfering in my life, Mom."

"Look, Lauren, I know you're not very happy with me right now, and I'm sorry about that. But I'm your mother, like it or not. And it's not *interference* for me to call your teacher and tell him there's a conflict. I wanted him to know you wouldn't miss the math session unless it was for something really important."

"So you told him I was going to see a *shrink?*" Lauren knew she was being unreasonable. After all, Matt had talked to her about a therapist. It was no news to *him* that she was screwed up. But her mother didn't know that.

Her mother looked at her, that look that made Lauren nervous, the one that made her feel her mother could read her mind.

Finally she sighed and said, "Honey...can we be honest with each other?"

"Sure, we can be honest. You start first. You tell me *why you're getting a divorce!*"

The silence lasted so long Lauren almost gave in and broke it. But she forced herself not to. The ball was in her mother's court, dammit. Let *her* say something.

At long last, her mother nodded. "All right, Lauren.

You win. The truth is, your father has done something I cannot forgive. It's not my place to tell you what. That's *his* place. If you really want to know, ask him to tell you."

Lauren stared at her mom.

"And there's something else you need to know," her mother said, her green eyes glittering the way they did when she was passionate about something, "as long as we're being honest with each other. We are going to have to sell this house and move into something much smaller and less expensive. And if you want to know why, you can ask your father about that, too!"

And then, shocking Lauren, her mother left the room and walked down the hall toward her bedroom.

A few moments later, Lauren heard her mother's bedroom door slam shut.

Chapter Four

"Lauren?"

Lauren blinked. "Oh, I'm sorry. I—I was daydreaming."

Dr. Pennington smiled. "My patients seem to do that often. Maybe I need to work on being less boring."

"You're not boring. I just started thinking about what you said, and…I don't know. My mind drifted off."

"Well, let's get back to your mother. How did you feel when she walked away from you like that?"

Lauren shrugged. "I don't know."

Dr. Pennington didn't say anything.

"It…it bothered me," Lauren finally admitted.

"In what way?"

"It seemed childish. Not like my mother at all." When the doctor didn't comment, Lauren sighed. "I'm the one who usually walks away."

Dr. Pennington nodded. "What happened after that?"

"Nothing."

"Nothing?"

"Well, I went to bed, and I guess my mom did, too. I didn't hear her after that."

"And what about the next morning? Did the two of you talk?"

Lauren shook her head. "Not about anything important. She asked me what I wanted for breakfast, and reminded me about my appointment with you and that was about it."

"Did that disappoint you?"

Lauren shrugged. She didn't want to admit that she *had* been disappointed. She'd wanted her mother to say she was sorry for trying to get Lauren to think the divorce was her dad's fault, but it hadn't happened.

"Are you going to talk to your father the way your mother suggested you should?" the doctor asked after a long moment of silence.

"I don't know." Lauren bit her lip. "Do *you* think I should?"

"It's not my place to say, Lauren," the doctor said gently.

"You *do* think I should."

"It never hurts to talk about the things that confuse us."

Lauren sighed. "I've tried to talk to him, you know, but he just keeps saying he'll explain everything some-day."

"How does that make you feel? When he evades your question?"

Without warning, Lauren's eyes filled with tears. "It makes me mad! Why do they both treat me like I'm a baby? I'm *not* a baby. This divorce affects me, too, you know. Why can't they understand that?"

Dr. Pennington's dark eyes were sympathetic. "I'm sure they do understand that, Lauren."

"Then why won't they *talk* to me?"

"Well, there could be any number of reasons. I know as a parent myself, I want to be strong for my children. I don't want to expose my weaknesses. Sometimes parents make mistakes or do things they're ashamed of, and it's difficult to admit that to a child. I'm not saying that's the case here, I'm just saying that's a possibility."

Lauren nodded glumly and brushed away her tears. "I guess I'll try to talk to my dad again, but I can't right now, because he's leaving today on a business trip. He won't be back for two weeks."

"That could be a good thing. By the time he comes home again, you'll have had some time to think about everything."

"Yeah, I guess so."

For the rest of the day and even after she was in bed that night, Lauren thought about her conversation with

Dr. Pennington. Was the doctor right? Was it possible that her dad really *had* done something her mother couldn't forgive? If he had, what could it be? Lauren knew it wasn't another woman, because her dad wasn't like that. He'd never have cheated on her mother the way Heather's father had done to *her* mother. So if it wasn't that, what else could be so bad that her mom wanted a divorce?

After several sessions with Dr. Pennington, Lauren finally accepted that nothing was going to bring her parents back together again, no matter how much she might want that to happen. And even though she still didn't know anything specific, she guessed she was okay with it. After all, it wasn't like she was the only kid whose parents were divorced. At least a third of the kids in her class seemed to come from broken homes.

She wasn't even sure she cared anymore about why they'd decided to split. Probably it was both their faults, and maybe it was better just to leave it at that.

"Lauren, if you're ready, I'll drop you at your father's."

Lauren looked up from her homework. She was spending the weekend with her dad, and she was looking forward to seeing him. She'd missed him while he was out of town, but he'd come home yesterday. They'd probably go out for a pizza or burger tonight. Maybe even go to a movie. "Okay." Gathering up her books, she stuffed them into a tote. She'd already packed her stuff for the weekend in a duffel bag, which was sitting by the back door. She pushed the kitchen chair back and stood. "I'm ready."

Her mother eyed her jeans and short-sleeved T-shirt. "Aren't you going to wear a jacket? It's chilly out."

Although it was the first week of April, the weather was anything but springlike. In fact, the temperature was supposed to go down to the mid-forties later tonight.

From habit, Lauren started to give her mother a smart answer, then caught herself. "It's in the mudroom." Dr. Pennington would be proud of her.

"Oh. Okay."

They didn't talk on the way to her dad's apartment, but it wasn't an uncomfortable silence. Lauren and her mom were still not back to the relationship they'd had before she'd told Lauren about the divorce, but things were better between them. Dr. Pennington had helped Lauren see that punishing her mom wasn't the solution to anything, that the only way Lauren was going to feel better was to try to understand that her parents were hurting as much as she was, that neither one was perfect, and that they were doing the best they could do under the circumstances.

"You're not a child, Lauren," Dr. Pennington had said. "You must know that we don't always get what we want, and we certainly don't get it by stamping our feet."

Lauren had felt bad when the doctor had said that.

Because that's what she *had* been doing, she realized. She'd been acting like a spoiled brat. She couldn't get her way, so she'd been pouting and saying ugly stuff and making life even harder for her mom *and* her dad.

Lauren knew her mom hated that they were going to have to sell the house. Her mom loved their house. She'd spent hundreds of hours painting and scraping and staining and scrubbing to make it the beautiful home it was now.

Lauren loved the house, too. But she guessed she'd survive the fact they had to move. On the positive side, she'd get to have a new room, and her mom had said she could decorate it any way she wanted to.

"Even if I want to paint it black?" Lauren had asked, testing the waters.

Her mom had smiled. "Even then."

Lauren *didn't* want to paint her new room black, but that wasn't the point.

Also on the positive side, she wouldn't have to change schools, because there was only one high school in Maple Hills.

"And we'll make sure we find a place that's fenced, so Trixie can play outside if she wants to," Lauren's mom had said.

So that was another plus. Lauren smiled, thinking how Dr. Pennington had told her that whenever something new happened or you were thinking about doing something different or changing something, you should make a list. On one side should be the cons—the bad stuff about the change—and on the other side should be the pros—the positive stuff. So far, Lauren's list about moving had more positives than negatives.

"Here we are, honey."

Lauren blinked. She'd been daydreaming again. She seemed to do a lot of that lately. Even Matt had noticed it. Lauren smiled again, thinking about Matt. So far, everything about him was a positive. Even the fact he was older wasn't a big deal. No, he was perfect.

She wondered if he had any idea how she felt about him. She thought he might, otherwise why was he spending so much time with her?

"I might not be there when you get home Sunday night," her mom said. "But I won't be real late. Zoe and I are going to the symphony. She got free tickets."

"Okay." Lauren got out of the car and waved goodbye.

Just like she'd thought, when she got inside, her dad said they were going to go out to eat.

"Oh, good," Lauren said happily. "Where are we going?"

"I thought we might try that new Chinese place on Elm Street."

"How soon are we going to leave? I'm starving." She plopped down onto a kitchen chair and put her duffel and homework on the table.

"Um, we'll go as soon as Alexandra gets here."

"Alexandra?"

"Yes, she's going to go to dinner with us."

Lauren grinned. "That's great! I've really missed her."

"So you like her?"

"Yeah, of course. She's cool."

Her dad pulled a chair out and sat across from her. His blue eyes were serious. "I'm glad you like her, honey, because there's something I've been meaning to tell you, and, well, it's better if I tell you before Alexandra gets here."

His expression suddenly made Lauren feel apprehensive.

"Alexandra and I…we, uh, we're seeing each other."

Lauren frowned. "*Seeing* each other? You mean, like, *dating?*"

"Yes."

Lauren couldn't take it in. Alexandra and her dad? When had they started *dating?* "H-how long has this been going on?"

"For a while now," he said, shrugging, acting like what he'd just told her wasn't a bombshell.

Lauren stared at him. "A while? But…all this time you've been telling me you wanted to come home."

He sighed. "We have to be realistic. That's not going to happen."

"Yes, I know that now, but I still don't understand. How could you be dating Alexandra *for a while* if that's what you were hoping?"

"I just…needed someone to talk to."

Something didn't feel right to Lauren. "Does Mom know about this?"

He hesitated, not meeting her eyes, then said, "Yes, your mother knows."

Lauren's heart began pounding. She couldn't believe what she was thinking, yet suddenly she knew it was true. Alexandra was the reason her mom and dad had split up. Alexandra and her dad had been seeing each other even *before* he'd left her mother. That's why her mother had thrown him out. That's why she'd told Lauren he'd done something she couldn't forgive.

Lauren stared at her dad, and he finally met her gaze. He didn't have to say the words out loud. Lauren could see the truth on his face.

Daddy…how could you?

It was a cry straight from her heart. She had always worshipped her father. He was her hero, the kind of man she hoped she'd marry some day.

And now….

She bit her lip. Remembered something she'd read once, about a hero having feet of clay. She was so disappointed, she felt sick.

"Lauren," he pleaded, "please don't look at me that way. It's not what you think."

Yes, it is. It's exactly what I think. Lauren didn't want to cry, but she could feel the tears threatening. She pushed her chair back and stood. "Dad, I'm sorry, but

I don't feel good. I don't think I can eat anything." In fact, the thought of food made her feel nauseous, even though only ten minutes ago she'd been starving. "I'm going to go lie down."

She didn't give him a chance to say anything, just gathered up her books and stuff, then bolted from the room. She barely made it to her room before the tears began streaming down her face.

Cheating. Her dad had been cheating on her mom. With Alexandra. It was like a soap opera. How had her mom found out? Had her dad told her?

She couldn't believe it. Her dad!

Lauren must have fallen asleep, because when she heard the knock on her bedroom door and glanced at the clock, she saw it was after nine.

Lauren didn't say anything. She was afraid it might be Alexandra knocking, and she didn't want to see her or talk to her. Not now. Not yet. In fact, she wasn't sure she ever wanted to see or talk to Alexandra again.

"Lauren."

Relief coursed through her. It was her dad. Slowly, she got up, switched on the bedside lamp, then walked over and unlocked the door.

He looked awful. His hair was all messy, as if he'd been running his hands through it, and his eyes…Lauren could hardly stand to look at his eyes. *I probably look like crap, too.*

"Can I come in?"

She shrugged. "Sure." She walked to the bed and sat on the edge. He sat next to her and reached for her hand. She let him take it, even though she didn't want to. "Where's Alexandra?" she said.

"She didn't come."

"Why not?"

"I called her and told her it wasn't a good idea."

"Good. I don't want to see that slut!"

"Lauren…"

"I mean it, Dad."

"Honey, look, will you let me explain?"

"What's to explain? I think I understand the situation."

"No, you don't. You're not old enough to understand."

"Oh, that's such *crap!*" She yanked her hand away. "I'm fifteen. I know all about sex. And I know all about *cheating!*" Angry tears spurted and she leaped up. "I want to go home."

"Lauren!" He got up, tried to put his arms around her.

"Don't," she sobbed. "Don't." She wrenched herself away from him. She tried to stop crying, but the harder she tried, the faster the tears came.

"All right, Lauren," he said in a sad voice.

Part of her wanted to say she was sorry, wanted her daddy to put his arms around her and tell her everything was okay. But the other part, the part that was reaching toward maturity and independence and thinking for herself, that part knew her childhood was over. Never again would she be Daddy's little girl who thought he was the perfect man.

Now she knew he had weaknesses and flaws.

And she also knew he'd done something awful to her mother.

And all these weeks, Lauren had been making it worse by being so ugly to her mother.

They didn't talk on the way to the house, but this time Lauren wasn't making lists or spinning daydreams. This time she was trying to come to terms with her new vision of her parents.

When they reached the house, he pulled up and into the driveway. Lauren opened the passenger side door.

"Lauren, wait…"

Lauren turned.

"I love you. You know that, don't you?"

She took a deep breath. "Yes."

"I can't stand it if you hate me."

"I don't hate you, Dad." *I'm just so disappointed in you.*

"I wish…" But he didn't finish.

Lauren nodded. There were lots of things she wished. Opening the door, she got out of the car. "Good night, Dad." She didn't look back.

Shawn and Matt had fallen into the habit of e-mailing each other. It had started after Lauren had agreed to see a therapist. Matt had e-mailed Shawn telling her about their conversation, and then Shawn had e-mailed him back to thank him.

He wrote back the next day and asked her if she wanted him to talk to the school counselor about possible therapists, and Shawn thanked him again and said that would be great, even though she intended to call their family physician and ask for her recommendations as well. Shawn closed her e-mail by saying she was late for her volunteer job, but would check back with him later that day.

When she returned from the Maple Hills Women's Center, where she had worked three days a week for more than four years, there was another e-mail waiting for her. He gave her a couple of names of family therapists that Mrs. Adler had given him. At the end he wrote, What kind of volunteer work do you do?

So she wrote back and told him all about the center. How she'd started by bringing a donation of clothes and books and how she'd seen a notice on their bulletin board about needing someone to answer the phones a few hours a day. Now I'm practically their office manager on the days I'm there, she wrote.

That should help you in your job hunt, he said in his answering e-mail, because she'd told him she was going to have to try to find paying work.

I hope so, she answered. I'm not actively looking yet, though. I'm waiting until the divorce is final.

When will that be? he asked.

Rick signed the papers two weeks ago, so it's just another seventeen days before the final decree comes through, she wrote back.

Before Shawn knew it, they were e-mailing every day, talking about all kinds of things that weren't even remotely related to Lauren.

When she'd told him her fears about finding a good job, he'd suggested she sign up for some computer courses.

That's a great idea, she'd written back. Thank you!

She found herself thinking about him a lot. He was so nice, and he was fun to talk to, even if the talking was electronic, maybe *especially* because the talking was electronic. She found it so easy to tell him things—the kinds of things she'd only told girlfriends before.

"It's weird," she told her Wednesday-night group. "But I feel as if we've been friends forever."

"Better watch it, Shawn," Ann said. "You're ripe for a rebound romance."

Shawn had just taken a bite of her burger. She was glad because it gave her time to think before replying. "He's just a friend. There's no romantic thing going on here."

Zoe grinned. "Really?"

"Really."

Zoe turned to Ann. "You should see this guy, Ann. He's cute and he's *very* sexy."

"He's also way younger than I am," Shawn said. Oh, she could kill Zoe sometimes.

"How much younger?" Carol asked. "Maybe he's the right age for Emma."

Now Shawn nearly choked. "He's too old for Emma," she sputtered, glad Emma hadn't been able to make it that evening.

"How old *is* he?" Susan asked.

"I don't know," Shawn admitted, "but I'm guessing about twenty-nine or thirty."

"And you're, what? Thirty-eight?" Zoe said.

"Almost thirty-nine."

"So? Ten years is nothing. You look younger than thirty-nine, anyway," Zoe said.

"Look, he's not interested in me. He just thinks of me as Lauren's mother."

"Oh, come on," Carol scoffed. "You're smart, pretty and sexy. You can bet he doesn't just think of you as Lauren's mother."

"Will you guys cut it out?" Shawn said. But secretly she was pleased. *Did* Matt think she was pretty? *And sexy. Don't forget sexy.*

They all laughed and continued to tease her.

"Let's give her a break," Ann said after awhile. "Maybe Shawn isn't ready to think about dating."

"I'm not," Shawn said gratefully. And yet she continued to mull over what they'd said. And she finally admitted to herself that she was drawn to Matt, and not just because he'd been kind and concerned about Lauren. Shawn would have liked him even if she'd met him somewhere else, under different circumstances.

But, she thought regretfully, he really *was* too young for her. Zoe might think ten years was nothing, but Shawn knew better. When he was forty, in the prime of his life, she'd be fifty, heading downhill.

No, it would never work.

Besides, he wasn't interested in her.

End of story.

Shawn hadn't even gotten the phone back in its base after calling the local community college about their computer classes when it rang. The caller ID showed this call was from Stella Vogel.

Shawn pressed the on button. "Hi, Stella."

Stella laughed. "I'll never get used to caller ID. I'm always taken aback when people answer using my name."

Shawn smiled. "Personally, I love knowing who's on the other end. I don't have to use my answering machine to screen my calls anymore."

"Speaking of screening calls, my office manager gave her notice yesterday. She's leaving in two weeks."

"Jane's *quitting?*"

"Yes, unfortunately. Her husband is being transferred to his company's Atlanta office."

"That's too bad. I know how much you depend on her."

"I hate losing her, but I'm glad for her, too. This new position is a great opportunity for her husband. Anyway, I was wondering…would you be interested in filling in here until I can find a replacement for her?"

"Me? Stella, I'd love to, but I don't have any experience in the legal field and the only office experience I have is at the women's center."

"I know that. It doesn't matter. I just need someone intelligent and well-spoken to answer the phone and field my calls as well as do a little typing and filing. You type, don't you?"

"Yes."

"Any experience using a computer?"

"Well, I use the one we have here at the house and the one at the center, but I've never learned any of the complicated stuff."

"If you could come in this week and next, Jane can teach you the basics."

"Well…" Shawn really wanted to do it, but it scared her, too. What if she completely messed up?

"Please, Shawn. I'm in a bind here."

"Well, as long as you don't expect too much."

"I'm not worried. You'll be fine."

By the time they'd hung up, Shawn had promised to be at Stella's office at eight the following morning. This would be fun, she decided, determined to think positively. And maybe it would give her some confidence in her own job hunt, not to mention a reference if she did a decent job for Stella.

Being away all day was going to present some challenges, though. First and foremost, there was Trixie. The dog could now go about six hours before having to be walked, but Shawn would be gone from the house more than nine hours. And Lauren was sometimes gone that long, too, especially when she had soccer practice or her team was being coached for the math competition.

Shawn sighed. She guessed she could come home for lunch. Stella's office was only ten minutes away.

The other problem was the house. She'd intended to get it shipshape this week in preparation for putting it on the market. But she guessed she could hold off for another couple of weeks.

For the rest of the day, she did as much as she could to get ready: she grocery shopped, she did the laundry, she ironed, and she even managed to squeeze in a haircut.

That night when Lauren got home after soccer practice, Shawn told her about the job.

Lauren grinned. "Mom, that's great. What's she going to pay you?"

Shawn laughed. "I didn't even ask."

"Mom…"

"I know. I should have. But the money isn't the most

important thing, not with this job, anyway." Shawn went on to explain about having a legitimate reference.

"You already have legitimate references. What about Mrs. Crosley at the women's center?"

Anita Crosley was the current director and the woman under whom Shawn worked.

"She'll be a good one, but you have to remember, that's a volunteer job."

"So? What you do there is just as important as any paying job."

Shawn walked over and hugged Lauren. "Thanks for your confidence in me, honey."

Later, after Lauren had gone up to her room to study, Shawn picked up the phone to call her girlfriends. Zoe thought this job would give Shawn great experience, a sentiment echoed by Ann and Carol. Susan wasn't home, so Shawn left a message for her. Then, instead of putting the phone down, she impulsively dialed Matt's number.

"Hey, guess what?" she said when he answered. She proceeded to tell him about the job with Stella.

"Shawn, that's terrific."

"It *is,* isn't it?"

"It'll be a great reference for you."

"I know."

"Plus it'll give you some confidence."

She laughed. "Are you reading my mind?"

He laughed, too. "I'm sorry. I'm so used to being a teacher, it's hard to turn it off sometimes."

They talked a while longer. Before saying goodbye, Matt made her promise to call or e-mail him the next day and let him know how her first day had gone.

Shawn thought about him for a long time after hanging up. Why was it she felt so comfortable with him? Was it because she knew they were just friends and she didn't have to worry about any sexual connotations?

That had to be it.

And yet…

Be honest. You know you like him…and not just as a friend, either.

Well, maybe she did. But it didn't matter because he didn't know that.

And he never would.

Chapter Five

The next morning, Shawn was ready to go before seven. She'd dressed carefully with an eye to how Jane had dressed for the job.

"Mom, you look nice," Lauren said when she came down for breakfast.

Shawn was wearing black pants, a tailored white blouse, and a gray-and-white herringbone jacket. Black pumps, silver button earrings and a silver bracelet completed her outfit.

After giving Lauren instructions about making sure Trixie was in her crate before she left for school ("I'll come home at noon to let her out for a while," Shawn promised), Shawn left for Stella's office.

The morning flew by. Between answering the phone, learning the word-processing program (they used WordPerfect whereas the only program Shawn had ever used was Word), and getting used to the filing system, Shawn was so busy she didn't have time to worry about whether she was doing a good job or anything else.

At noon, they closed the office for an hour. Stella asked Shawn if she wanted to grab a burger at Callie's, but Shawn explained about Trixie.

"The dog might present a problem if you end up having to drive into the city every day," Stella said.

"Anyplace we move will have to have a fenced yard so she can be outdoors." But Shawn was worried. During the worst of the winter months, it would be too cold for the dog to stay out all the time. For at least the hundredth time, she wished Rick hadn't bought the dog for Lauren. Now both she *and* Lauren were so attached to Trixie, she couldn't even imagine getting rid of her.

Well, she'd just have to cross that bridge when she came to it, she thought as she drove home.

While there, Shawn ate a tuna-salad sandwich, then took an apple with her when she walked Trixie. She made it back to the office with five minutes to spare.

The afternoon was even busier than the morning, and by the end of the day, Shawn was tired but exhilarated.

"You did great today," Jane said.

"Thanks." Shawn *was* pleased with herself. She hadn't made any gigantic mistakes, at least none that she knew of, and she'd caught on to the word-processing program easily. In fact, she'd typed a brief and several letters, and Jane had pronounced them perfect.

By the time the two weeks of Jane's notice were up, Shawn felt she could adequately fill in at the office until Stella found a permanent replacement.

But that afternoon, Stella surprised Shawn by saying, "Jane says you're a marvel, that you've caught on to everything so quickly and have done such an amazing job, I'd be crazy not to hire you." She named a salary that was at the upper end of what Shawn had hoped to get.

Shawn was so thrilled she hardly knew what to say. She loved working for Stella and being able to work in Maple Hills so close to home…. What could *be* more perfect?

She couldn't wait to call her girlfriends and Matt. The women were all happy for her, saying they'd celebrate on Wednesday night at Callie's.

"This calls for a celebration," Matt said, echoing their sentiments. "How about if I take you out to dinner tomorrow night? Unless you have plans?"

Shawn was taken aback by the invitation, so it took her a minute to say no, she didn't have plans. As soon as the words were out of her mouth, she wondered if this was a smart thing to be doing.

Oh, for heaven's sake, it's just dinner with a friend. Just like the dinners you have on Wednesday nights with your girlfriends.

"Great," he said. "How about Italian food? Do you like Tony's?"

Shawn said she loved Tony's.

"I'll pick you up at seven, that okay?"

"Um, I could just meet you there."

"Shawn, don't be silly. Why should we *both* drive?"

Because if we both drive, then it's not a date.

But she couldn't say that out loud, so she ended by agreeing that he could come by at seven.

After they hung up, she told herself not to make a big deal out of this, it wasn't a date. It was just two friends going to dinner to celebrate her new job.

Even so, she was glad Lauren would be spending tomorrow night with Rick and Alexandra. She knew without being told that Lauren wouldn't like it, no matter how Shawn explained they were only friends.

"Who was that, Mom?" Lauren said.

Shawn jumped. She hadn't heard Lauren walk up behind her. "I—I was just calling everyone to tell them about the job." That wasn't a lie. She *had* been calling everyone.

"I'll bet they were happy for you, huh?"

"Yes." Damn. Why did she feel so guilty?

"Is it okay if I tell Dad?"

"Of course. Why wouldn't it be?"

Lauren shrugged. "I don't know."

"Look, Lauren, I don't want you to feel you have to hide anything from your father…or from Alexandra, for that matter. You can talk to them about anything you want." There'd been enough hiding and subterfuge and lying, Shawn thought. She wanted everything above-board from now on. She ignored the twinge of guilt. She was going to tell Lauren about Matt. Just not right now.

"I could care less about talking to Alexandra," Lauren said.

"Honey…"

"I know. She's Dad's girlfriend." Lauren made a face. "I don't like her anymore, Mom."

Shawn sighed. "I know. But for your dad's sake, you'll have to try, because I think this is probably important to him."

Lauren picked at a loose thread on her sweater. When her eyes met Shawn's again, they were serious. "You know what your trouble is, Mom? You're too nice."

Shawn couldn't help smiling. "That's the nicest thing anyone's said to me in a long time."

The next day, after Lauren left for Rick's, Shawn looked over the clothes in her closet. Tony's wasn't a fancy place, so she decided her new jeans and a white blouse would be a perfectly fine outfit. Anything dressier might send the wrong message, like she *might* be considering this a date.

But then she worried that Matt might be dressed up, and she'd look foolish in her jeans, so when it was time to get ready, she put on a long denim skirt and instead of the blouse, paired it with a white summer sweater. She was glad she'd made the change when Matt arrived, because he *was* kind of dressed up in nice khaki pants and a dark brown knit shirt. "Wow," he said, eyeing her. "You look great."

"Thanks." She wanted to say she thought he looked great, too, but she felt suddenly shy and awkward. Besides, this *wasn't* a date.

He drove a Jeep, which made Shawn smile. It was such a *young* man's car. *Well, he is young, remember?*

"My sister introduced me to Tony's," he said once they were on their way.

"Your sister? Does your family live here, then?"

"Only the one sister and her husband and kids. They moved here a little over a year ago."

"I didn't think you were from around here."

"No. Born and raised in Cleveland."

"This is quite a change, then."

"Yeah, it is."

"What made you decide to leave Cleveland?"

It was a moment before he answered. "Like you, I went through a painful breakup."

"Oh. I'm sorry." Did that mean he was divorced?

As if he'd read her mind, he said, "We weren't married. We were engaged. Then she found someone who made a lot more money than a teacher and decided she didn't love me after all."

"She was a fool."

He chuckled. "Maybe not. It's true I couldn't give her the things she wanted."

"But she must have known that when you got engaged."

"It really doesn't matter. I'm over it. Breaking up with Sarah was probably the best thing for both of us. Thing is, I want kids. And she was never sure she did."

"You're probably right, then. It *was* the best thing. So do you like living here?"

"I like it a lot."

"It's very different than the city, though."

"Yeah, but it's close enough to Columbus that it doesn't matter. Here I've got the best of both worlds. City attractions if I want them, and small-town living when I don't."

His grin was infectious. So was his enthusiasm.

"How long have *you* lived here?" he asked.

"We moved to Maple Hills when we had Lauren."

"Where were you living before that?"

"In Columbus."

By now they'd reached the restaurant. The parking lot was crowded. "Have you been here before?" he asked.

Shawn smiled. "It's one of my favorite places to eat." She was afraid they would have a wait tonight, but when they got inside, Tess, the hostess, immediately led them to a table, saying, "You're in luck. This is the last empty table."

They were seated, with glasses of water and menus in front of them, and had given their waitress their drink orders, when a pretty, brown-haired woman approached their table.

"Matt!" she said. "Hi. I didn't know you were coming here tonight."

"Cathy," he said. He smiled and got up, giving the woman a hug.

The woman gave Shawn a curious look.

"Cathy," he said, "I'd like you to meet Shawn Fletcher. Shawn, this is my sister Cathy Dickson."

Shawn stood, too. Now that she knew the woman was Matt's sister, she could see the resemblance, especially around the eyes and mouth. "You look familiar to me," she said.

"And you to me," Cathy said.

They studied each other for a moment. Shawn couldn't place Matt's sister immediately. Then it dawned on her. "Lucy's Salon," she said. "You were getting a haircut this morning."

Cathy smiled. "Yes, I was. And you were getting a manicure."

"Are Lowell and the kids here?" Matt asked.

Cathy shook her head. "Nope. He's babysitting. I'm here with a couple of the other teachers."

"Oh, you're a teacher, too?" Shawn asked.

"Yes. I teach kindergarten at Elm Street Elementary."

"That's the school my daughter attended."

"Shawn's the mother of one of my best math students," Matt explained.

"Oh." She gave Matt a funny look. "Well, I'd better be getting back to my group. It was nice to meet you, Shawn."

"You, too."

"See you later, Matt."

Once she was gone, Matt said, "Well, I'll be in for it now."

"What do you mean?"

"My sister is a champion matchmaker. She thinks it's high time I got married, and she's been trying to fix me up with one of her female friends ever since I got here. She'll want to know every last detail about you."

Shawn felt decidedly uncomfortable under his warm gaze. She wanted to say *but I'm not a romantic interest, I'm just a friend, and you'll have to set her straight,* but the words wouldn't come out of her mouth. "You're still young," she finally managed to say. "You've got time."

"Not that young. I'm already thirty-two. All my siblings except for my younger sister Amy are already married. And Amy's engaged. She's getting married this summer."

Thirty-two. Not quite as young as Shawn had thought. But still too young for her.

"How old were you when you got married?" he asked.

"Twenty. Which is way too young. I hope Lauren waits until she's at least in her late twenties."

Just then their waitress brought their wine and a basket of warm focaccia bread. "Ready to order?" she said.

"I am," Matt said. "What about you, Shawn?"

"I know what I want."

Once they'd placed their orders—lasagna for Matt and chicken marsala for Shawn—Matt said, "I *thought* you were a child bride. I figured you couldn't be much older than I am, yet you've got a fifteen-year-old daughter."

"I'll be thirty-nine on my next birthday," Shawn said. Might as well get it out in the open.

He shook his head. "Hard to believe. I thought you were younger than me when I first met you."

"Oh, come on…" But she was flattered because she could see he was serious. She took a piece of focaccia bread. It smelled wonderful.

"No, seriously, I did."

"Well, thank you."

"Now, tell me about the job. What's it like in a law office?"

So while they waited for their salads, Shawn talked about her experiences at Stella's office. Then the salads came and the subject turned to teaching.

"I really admire teachers," Shawn said. "It seems such a thankless job so much of the time."

"Only some of the time. I find being a teacher really rewarding." He popped a cherry tomato into his mouth. "Most days, anyway."

"Did you always want to teach?"

He shook his head. "Nope. I wanted to be a major-league pitcher."

Shawn laughed. "The typical male fantasy." She ate a piece of cucumber.

He grinned. "Yep."

"I wanted to be a ballerina."

"The typical female fantasy."

"Except girls nowadays want to be pop singers."

"Some of them, maybe. Not all."

"Really?" Shawn said, thinking of Lauren, whose bedroom was plastered with posters of girl singers with names like Britney and Ashlee and Christina.

By now their entrées had come, and for a while, they dug in. The chicken marsala was delicious, and from the way Matt was attacking his lasagna, he seemed to share her enthusiasm for the food here.

"I'm glad to see you have a good appetite," he said. "A lot of women just pick at their food."

"I don't eat like this all the time."

"I don't, either." He laughed. "Sometimes I just have a bowl of cereal for dinner."

"Me, too!" Shawn said. "Rick—" She stopped. "My ex always thought I was nuts because I enjoy having breakfast at night."

"If you tell me you also eat cold pizza for breakfast, I may just have to marry you."

"Well, there we're different," she said lightly, "because cold pizza would be the *last* thing I'd want in the morning." God, he had gorgeous eyes.

"Should I take that as a no?"

Shawn knew he was joking. Even so, she was uncomfortable. The trouble was, she was so out of practice with this kind of banter. She was relieved to see their waitress approach to clear the table.

Neither wanted coffee or dessert, so while Matt paid the bill, Shawn went to the ladies' room. When she came out, he was standing by the door waiting for her. He smiled. "Ready?"

They didn't talk much on the way back to Shawn's, but it was a friendly silence. Shawn was thinking how much she'd enjoyed the evening and how nice it had been to go to dinner with an attractive man. It really was too bad that he was so much younger, for she knew, after tonight, that she could really like him.

Maybe if it were just her…

But it wasn't just her. There was Lauren to consider. And Shawn knew instinctively that Lauren would not like it if she thought Shawn was interested in Matt.

Forget it. He's too young for you, and that's that.

When they reached the house, Matt pulled up and into the driveway. Shawn was glad she'd left the outside lights on as well as a lamp in the living room. There was nothing she hated more than going into an empty house. Of course, Trixie was there, so it wasn't completely empty. She smiled, thinking of Trixie.

"What are you smiling about?" he asked.

"Oh, just thinking about our dog. Do you like dogs?"

"I love dogs. In fact, I'm thinking of getting one. What kind of dog do you have?"

"Trixie's really not mine. Lauren's father gave her the dog on her birthday back in September. She's a chocolate Lab. I was really against it, but now I've fallen in love with her, too."

"Labs are my favorite dog."

"Really?" Impulsively, she said, "Do you want to come in and meet Trixie? I'll have to walk her before I go to bed. Maybe you could walk with us."

"I'd love to."

What are you doing, Shawn? Shawn ignored her inner voice. After all, walking a dog was a perfectly innocent pastime.

Trixie was ecstatic when Shawn let her out of her crate and picked up her lead. The dog started jumping and barking.

Matt laughed. "She knows she's going out."

"She loves to go for a walk."

"Here, let me," he said, taking the lead from Shawn and fastening it to Trixie's collar.

They walked around the block. It was a beautiful evening, breezy but not cold. At one point, they met an older couple who were walking arm in arm in the opposite direction.

"Hello," the older woman said. She smiled at them. "What a beautiful dog you've got."

The older gentleman knelt to pet Trixie.

After they'd gone on their way, Matt said, "People in this town are so friendly."

"Yes," Shawn said. She wondered what the older couple had thought of them. Had they imagined she and Matt were married? That they were walking their dog before going to bed? Just the thought made her feel flustered. *What is* wrong *with you? Why do you keep thinking such inappropriate things? You're acting like a silly teenager.*

The trouble was, Matt was too darned attractive. And she was attracted to him. No denying that.

When they got back to the house, they walked around back. At the door, he gave the lead to Shawn. "I had a great time tonight."

"Me, too. Thank you."

"I hope we can do it again soon."

Shawn knew she should say something. Something to make it clear that they were just friends. And that friends was all they'd ever be. Instead, she heard herself say, "I'd like that."

Oh, Shawn, she thought as she watched him walk back down the driveway, *you're playing with fire. And people who play with fire always get burned.*

When Lauren came home the following afternoon, she seemed subdued.

"What's wrong, honey? Did something happen?" Shawn asked.

Lauren's eyes met hers. "Dad and Alexandra are going to get married next weekend, and he wants me to be there."

Shawn wasn't sure why the news should send a pang shooting through her. She no longer loved Rick, and she had known he and Alexandra would probably end up together once the divorce was final. But still…she and Rick had been married a long time. And it was so soon…the divorce had only become final two weeks ago. "Well, how do you feel about that?"

Lauren shrugged. "I really don't want to go."

"Where are they getting married?" Shawn asked, stalling for time.

"In Columbus. By a justice of the peace."

"I think you should go."

"You do?"

"Yes. I think, if you don't, you'll always be sorry. Your dad loves you. Our divorce doesn't change that. And Alexandra is going to be his wife. You *should* be there." Walking over to her daughter, Shawn put her arm around Lauren's shoulder. "It'll be okay."

Lauren bit her lip.

"It will."

"And you…don't care if I go?"

"Of course not. Why would I?"

Lauren shrugged again. "I don't know. I just thought—"

"I don't care at all. In fact, I want you to go."

"You do?"

"Yes."

For a moment, Lauren didn't say anything. Then she blurted, "I love you, Mom."

Shawn's eyes filled with tears. "Oh, sweetheart, I love you, too."

Chapter Six

Matt always went to Cathy and Lowell's for Sunday dinner, and normally he enjoyed it. Today, however, he knew he'd be in for the third degree. If he could have come up with a plausible excuse not to go, he would have, because Cathy had an uncanny knack of seeing things he didn't want her to see. But he couldn't think of a thing she'd buy, so promptly at one, he headed for his sister's house.

Just as he'd thought, the first thing Cathy said when Matt walked into the kitchen was "So how long have you been seeing this Shawn and why didn't you *tell* me you were dating someone? If you *had,* I wouldn't have been trying so hard to fix you up on blind dates."

"What happened to *hi, bro, glad to see you*," Matt said dryly.

Her husband, Lowell, who was standing at the kitchen counter tossing a salad, chuckled. "Never let it be said Cathy doesn't cut to the chase."

Matt rolled his eyes. "At least give me a drink first, then I'll answer your questions."

"What do you want?" Lowell asked. "I'll get it."

"How about a nice cold beer?"

"In that case, why don't you grab one from the fridge?" Lowell invited.

"So quit stalling," Cathy said. She lifted the lid on a big pot. The aroma of tomatoes and garlic rose on a bed of steam. "How long have you been seeing her?"

"Last night was our first date," Matt said as casually as he could manage. "And what's that you're making? It smells great."

"Chicken cacciatore, and don't change the subject."

"I'm not. I told you. Last night's the first time we've been out."

"And she's the mother of one of your students?"

"One of my best students."

Cathy frowned.

"What?"

"So Shawn's what? Divorced?"

"Yes."

"She doesn't look old enough to have a fifteen-year-old."

Matt smiled. "I know. That's what I told her."

"How old *is* she?"

"Cathy..." Lowell said warningly.

"No, it's okay, Lowell." Turning to his sister, Matt said, "She's almost thirty-nine. And before you say she's too old for me, she's not."

"I wasn't going to say that."

"The heck she wasn't," Lowell said. He winked at Matt.

Cathy gave Lowell a look that said *keep out of this*. "I wasn't! Still...if you two *should* get serious about each other, well..."

"We've only had one date," Matt pointed out. He took a handful of cashews from the crystal bowl sitting on the table and popped a few into his mouth.

"But what if you *do* end up liking her a lot and getting serious?" Cathy said.

"What if I do?"

"Well, a woman who is practically in her forties and who already has a teenaged daughter is probably not going to want to even *think* about having another child." Cathy put down the wooden spoon she'd been using and turned to face him. "And I thought you really wanted kids, Matt."

"I do want kids."

"Then is Shawn a wise choice?"

"Look, Cathy, I know you're just being a big sister, but none of this is really your—"

Just then, Stacy, Cathy and Lowell's fourteen-year-old, walked into the kitchen, and Matt stopped before finishing his sentence. But he could see Cathy had gotten the message.

"Uncle Matt!" Stacy said. "I didn't know you were here." She walked over and gave him a hug.

"Hello, squirt."

She grinned. "When're you going to stop using that silly baby name?"

"Never. I don't want you to grow up."

"No one in this family wants me to grow up," she grumbled.

"If you were smart, you wouldn't want to, either," Lowell said. "Being a grown-up is not all it's cracked up to be."

"Oh, Dad..." Turning to her mother, she said, "When's dinner? I'm starving."

"In about twenty minutes. Why don't you set the table? By the time you're done, I'll be ready."

Stacy sighed elaborately, but she went to do Cathy's bidding.

If Matt had thought the subject of Shawn was finished, he was wrong, for Cathy—in a much lower tone since Stacy was in hearing distance—said, "Look, Matt, I'm sorry if I'm out of bounds, but you're my brother. I care about you."

Lowell grinned. "You might as well give up, Matt. There's no privacy in this family."

"Shawn's just a friend, anyway," Matt said. He wouldn't have admitted it for the world, but Cathy's observation that Shawn probably wouldn't want more children gave him pause. He *did* want kids. What would he do if he and Shawn became serious about each other and he had to choose? Shawn…or children of his own?

Maybe, as Cathy had suggested, the smartest thing he could do was forget about Shawn.

Zoe called Shawn at noon on Sunday to see if she might want to catch a movie that afternoon.

"What's playing?" Shawn asked. She knew she shouldn't go out. She had laundry waiting, and she'd planned to cook a couple of meals for them to have during the week.

"There's that new Orlando Bloom movie at AMC."

Shawn smiled. "I know. You salivate over Orlando Bloom."

"Well, you've gotta admit he's gorgeous."

"I really should stay home and get some stuff done. I'm a working girl now, you know."

"Oh, come on, Shawn. Emma's gone to spend a study weekend with Lisa, and I'm bored. It'll just be a couple of hours."

Shawn wavered. Lauren wouldn't be home before five, and the laundry could wait until tonight. "Oh, okay. What time does the movie start?"

"Ten minutes after two. I'll swing by for you about one-forty, okay?"

Shawn decided she'd better let Lauren know where she'd be just in case she didn't make it home before her daughter, so she called Lauren's cell phone.

"Okay, Mom," Lauren said when Shawn told her about the movie with Zoe. "Have fun. I'll see you later."

Shawn *did* have fun. The movie was good, and Zoe was always great company. Afterward, she wanted to grab a burger at Callie's.

Shawn grimaced. "I can't, Zoe. Lauren'll be home soon. Besides, I've got some chicken thighs and mush-rooms cooking in the Crock-Pot. Why don't you come and eat with us?"

"You talked me into it," Zoe said.

Shawn had been debating whether or not to tell Zoe about the dinner out with Matt. She was dying to talk about him with someone, and Zoe always had sensible advice. But she would hate to be in the middle of a con-versation about him when Lauren got home. But when Shawn checked her cell phone, there was a message from Lauren saying she wouldn't be home till six and was that okay? Shawn immediately called her back and said it was fine. "Zoe's coming to dinner with us," she added.

"Oh, good," Lauren said. "See you later."

When Shawn and Zoe got to the house, Shawn poured Zoe a glass of merlot and put her to work making a salad. Shawn put rice on to cook, checked the chicken, then poured herself a glass of wine and began to chop up a tomato for the salad. Casually, she said, "Matt took me to dinner last night to celebrate my new job."

Zoe stopped tearing lettuce leaves and stared at Shawn. "Oh, really?"

Shawn ignored the suggestive tone, saying only, "Yeah, it was fun. We went to Tony's."

When Zoe didn't say anything, Shawn finally looked at her. "Say something."

Zoe only smiled.

"I hate it when you look at me like that."

"Like what?" Zoe said innocently. "Like, I knew you were interested in him, so why have you been denying it?"

"It wasn't even a date, Zoe. He was just being nice because of the job."

"You keep telling yourself that, Shawn."

"Look, we're just friends."

Zoe resumed tearing lettuce leaves. "There are very few real friendships between men and women, you know."

"You're such a cynic."

"I'm not a cynic. I'm a realist."

"Not every male/female relationship revolves around sex."

Zoe snorted.

"Well, they *don't*."

Finishing with the lettuce, Zoe began to chop up some baby carrots. "Tell me something, Shawn. Can you honestly say you've never even thought of him in terms of sexual attraction?"

Shawn wanted to say no, she hadn't, but she was not a good liar. "Of course, I have, but he's too young for me, and I know it."

Zoe smiled. "And does *he* know it?"

"Of course he does." But Shawn knew she didn't sound convinced, and she knew Zoe realized it, too.

Zoe put down the knife she'd been using and turned to face Shawn. There was no trace of teasing in her voice. "Look, Shawn, if you really think he's all wrong for you, then the smart thing to do would be not to go out with him again."

Shawn nodded. She knew Zoe was right.

But she couldn't help a regretful sigh. And she still hoped she could figure out a way to keep Matt as a friend, yet let him know that if he *did* want more, it wasn't a good idea for either of them, without ruining the friendship.

The question was how?

The day of the wedding dawned sunny and mild. Rick and Alexandra were picking Lauren up and would be there at ten. Shawn had taken Lauren shopping earlier in the week to find a dress that was suitable for the wedding but would also be something she would enjoy wearing again. They'd found the perfect dress at a small boutique that had opened earlier that year. It was a sea-green silk crepe with tiny sleeves, a square neckline and a short fitted skirt. It complemented Lauren's eyes and hair and made her look older than her fifteen years, which thrilled her but made Shawn kind of sad. She didn't want Lauren to grow up. She wanted to keep her young and unspoiled forever.

On the dot of ten, Rick's car pulled into the driveway. Shawn kissed Lauren goodbye, then stood watching from the window as she got into the car and they drove away.

Shawn stood there for a long time, just thinking. And then, with a determined sigh, she forced herself to go upstairs and finish cleaning the master bathroom. The house was finally on the market, and this afternoon all the agents from Ann's realty company would be coming to preview the house. Shawn wanted it to look its best.

The trouble with cleaning was it gave you too much time to think. She was no longer thinking about the wedding, though. Now her thoughts had veered to Matt and how she was going to handle it if he invited her out again.

I'll just have to come right out and tell him he's too young for me. That we can't see each other anymore.

Oh, for heaven's sake. How could she do that? She'd feel like a fool.

Just because he'd flirted with her a little bit meant nothing. She had no real reason to think he viewed her as anything other than a friend. Why would he? He knew how old she was. He'd even told her he wanted kids. When he was ready for another committed relationship, he'd pick a young woman, because he was smart enough to know Shawn was well past the child-bearing stage. Oh sure, she realized there were women out there giving birth in their forties, but Shawn would never be one of them, even if she wanted to be. In fact, not having another child was one of the biggest disappointments in her and Rick's marriage. It wasn't that they hadn't tried. Both had wanted at least one more child. But it had never happened.

So, under the circumstances, why *couldn't* Shawn continue to see Matt?

What would be the harm?

Matt thought about Shawn a lot over the next two weeks. He had decided that despite what Cathy had said, whether or not Shawn could have more children or wanted more children was not important right now. What was important was exploring his feelings for her and seeing if she shared them.

But he knew he had to tread carefully because he didn't want to jinx his chances with her before they'd even begun. Whether he liked it or not, he knew Shawn wasn't ready for a relationship. It was too soon after her divorce. Yet he didn't want to take a chance on her meeting someone else while he was waiting for her to *be* ready, either.

So he compromised. He e-mailed her every day and he invited her to accompany him and the math team to the state competition as one of the parent chaperones.

"Oh, I wish I could," she said, "but I'm so new on my job. I couldn't ask for a day off."

"I'll bet your boss would understand."

"I'm sure she would, but I still don't want to do it."

Matt was disappointed. It would have been fun to have Shawn there and a way for him to spend time with her without making a big deal out of it.

"I'm sorry," she said.

"Me, too. It would have been fun having you along. Someone for me to hang with." Then he laughed. "How about making it up to me by letting me take you to a movie Friday night?"

"I can't, Matt. Lauren's going to be here this weekend."

"Surely she's old enough to stay on her own for an evening."

She didn't say anything for a moment. "You know she has a crush on you."

"Does she?" Lots of the girls developed crushes on him. It came with the territory. "Well, if she does, it'll pass. By next semester, she'll find someone else to have a crush on. Preferably, a boy her own age."

"But in the meantime, I think she'd be upset if she thought we were…you know…friends."

Lauren probably *would* be upset. But sooner or later, she would have to know that he and Shawn were seeing each other, because he didn't intend to go away.

"All right, Shawn. I understand. But I want a rain check."

After they hung up, Matt wondered if Shawn really did think of them as just friends.

He didn't think so.

He was pretty sure he'd felt the same vibes coming from her that he felt himself.

Still, if she *didn't* think of him in terms of a romantic relationship, maybe it was best to find out now, before his own feelings got any more involved.

Either that or he'd have to change her mind.

"Now are you *sure* you have everything?"

Lauren rolled her eyes. "Mahhh-om. You've asked me that three times already." Soon she would be leaving for Columbus and the state math competition, but her mom was acting as if she were leaving home for college or something. "I'm only gonna be gone two nights."

"I know." Her mom smiled sheepishly while digging in her purse. After a few seconds of searching, she pulled out her wallet. "I wish I was going along as a chaperone."

"I know. I do, too." But Lauren was secretly glad her mom *wasn't* going. Now, Lauren would be free to spend more time around Matt. If her mom had been going with them, Lauren would have had to spend her free time with her.

Her mom handed her several twenty-dollar bills. "Here's some extra money for you, just in case."

"Thanks, but I don't need it. I have enough from my babysitting." Lauren knew her mom needed every penny, especially until they were able to sell the house.

"No, you take it, Lauren. If you don't need it, great. But I don't want you to run short."

Lauren reluctantly took the money, but she was determined not to spend it. Sometimes she felt guilty about how nice her mom was and how hard she was trying to make things okay for them, because Lauren wasn't always nice in return. The trouble was, her mom got on her nerves when she hovered. Heather said all moms hover, it's part of the Mom Rules, but Lauren wasn't a baby anymore, and she wished her mom would realize that and give her some space.

Still, Lauren realized she was lucky. Her mom could have been a bitch like Francesca Lewis's mom. Lauren cringed, remembering how Francesca's mother had made a spectacle of herself at the mall the week before. Lauren knew Francesca had been mortified.

"Good luck, honey. I wish I could wait till your ride gets here, but I don't want to be late for work."

Lauren gave her mom a hug. "It's okay. You go on. I'll be fine."

"Call me tonight, okay?"

"Okay."

"I'll be thinking about you."

"I know."

Her mom kissed her cheek, then left. Lauren breathed a sigh of relief when her car pulled out of the driveway. Now Lauren was free to think about the weekend and Matt.

Matt.

Lauren's heart sped up just *thinking* about him. He was so cute. She wondered if he suspected how she felt about him. Sometimes she thought he did and other times she wasn't sure. She knew he liked her. That was obvious. He took a lot more interest in her than he did the other girls. And that wasn't her imagination, either. Just yesterday he'd gone out of his way to ask her how things were going and if she was feeling better about everything. Why would he even bother if he didn't care about her?

Lauren smiled thinking how she'd managed to make sure she rode in the same car as he did on the trip into Columbus. Not that it was such a long trip, but still… riding in the same car meant that much more time in his company.

She was still thinking about him when Mrs. Peabody—who was Jason Peabody's mother—pulled into the driveway. Jason, Lauren, Francesca Lewis and Raleigh Trumbull were the four sophomore students on the team. All were riding with Mrs. Peabody, and so was Matt.

Calling, "Bye, Trixie," in the direction of the dog's crate, Lauren grabbed her duffel bag, her purse, and the tote containing her study materials and was out the door in a flash.

She was disappointed to see that Matt was sitting up front in the passenger seat. She'd hoped Jason would be up there with his mother and Matt would be in the back. But it worked out okay, because Jason and Raleigh were sitting in the very back, and Francesca was already belted into the seat directly behind Matt, so Lauren sat behind Mrs. Peabody, which gave her a perfect view of Matt. And every time he turned around to say something, he was looking right at her. It was like he was speaking directly to her.

She was so happy, she wasn't sure she could stand it. The only way this trip could be better would be if she and Matt were by themselves.

They arrived at the hotel in record time, dumped their bags to be stored until their rooms were ready, then headed straight to the conference center where the competition was being held. The first round of testing would begin promptly at one o'clock, but there was time to grab a sandwich and a drink before they'd have to find their group.

Lauren maneuvered so that she was sitting across from Matt while they ate.

"So, are you guys nervous?" he asked, looking around at the group.

The boys laughed and said no way, piece of cake, what was there to be nervous about?

Francesca and Lauren were honest and admitted that, yes, they were nervous.

"Don't be," Matt said, looking directly at Lauren. "You're going to be great."

She knew he was telling her he thought *she* was great. *I think you're great, too,* she telegraphed with her eyes.

"Hey, Fletcher," Raleigh said. "You gonna be a counselor at Sunshine Camp this year?"

Lauren nodded reluctantly. "I'm supposed to." She was so torn about camp. She'd loved being a counselor last year, but this year she hated to be gone so much of the summer. She wouldn't get to see Matt!

"What kind of camp is it?" Matt asked.

"It's a camp for underprivileged children," Mrs. Peabody answered before Lauren could. "Sponsored by our church."

Lauren hated that about some adults. Matt had asked *her* the question, not Know-it-all Peabody.

"And you were a counselor there before?" Matt asked.

"Last year," Lauren said. Despite her indecision

about the coming summer, she smiled, remembering. "It was great. The kids are lots of fun, and I really liked doing it."

"Good for you," he said. "I used to be a camp counselor when I was your age, too."

She could see he was proud of her, and that made her decision for her. Of course she'd go again. She probably wouldn't have gotten to see much of Matt this summer, anyway. At least at camp she'd have lots of fun things to do and the summer would fly by.

And when she got back and school started again, she'd be only weeks away from turning sixteen. And then, in two *more* years, she'd be eighteen.

And then…

Her heart thumped as she met Matt's gaze. When he smiled, she knew, without a doubt, he was feeling the same things she was.

For the first time since her parents had split, Lauren felt completely happy.

The next day, Shawn kept thinking about Lauren and wondering how the team was doing. They'd talked briefly the night before, but the conversation hadn't been all that satisfying to Shawn. She could tell Lauren's mind was elsewhere, that she wanted to be off studying with her teammates or something, so Shawn had let her go after wishing her good luck.

She didn't have too much time to think, though, because the house was shown twice before two o'clock. An hour later, she had just put in a load of laundry and was thinking about mixing up a meat loaf when the phone rang.

"Shawn?" It was Ann. "Great news. We have an offer."

"We do?"

"Yes. The couple who looked at the house this afternoon. I'd like to bring the offer over for you to see."

"Is it a good one?" Shawn was afraid to hope.

"Not quite as good as we'd hoped, but there's room for negotiation, I think."

Shawn said to come over and Ann arrived less than twenty minutes later. After discussing the offer, they decided to counter. Shawn signed the papers and Ann left, promising to call her as soon as she knew anything.

Shawn tried not to dwell on the offer; nothing might come of it, but she couldn't help but hope.

She had just put the meat loaf in the oven when Ann called back.

"They accepted," she said jubilantly. "The only drawback is, they want occupancy by June 15th."

"Wow," Shawn said. It was already the second week of May. "I guess I'd better start looking for a place to move to right away."

"Don't worry. I already have two or three places in mind. I just didn't want to show them to you until we knew for sure that your house had sold."

They talked a while longer, then Ann said she could take Shawn out the following day, if she wanted.

Shawn danced around the kitchen after they'd hung up. Knowing the house was sold was such a relief. Now she wouldn't have to worry about money so much. She couldn't wait to tell Lauren.

Lauren called an hour later to say their team had placed second overall in the competition and she, herself, had come in seventh among all the sophomores competing.

"Oh, sweetheart," Shawn said, "I'm so proud of you."

"Thanks, Mom."

"So when are you leaving?"

"Pretty soon, but we'll probably not get there before nine or ten."

"Why not?"

"We're going to stop somewhere for dinner and celebrate."

"I have some good news, too." Shawn proceeded to tell Lauren about the house.

"That's great, Mom. When will we have to move?"

Shawn explained about what the buyers wanted. "Ann's taking me to look at houses tomorrow. Want to go?"

"I'd better not. I have a French test on Tuesday."

"But don't you want to help pick out a house?"

"I trust you. Anyway, I'll get to see whatever you like, won't I?"

Shawn smiled. Lauren was right. Shawn could cull the number down to serious contenders. "Of course, you will."

After they hung up, Shawn felt better about the future than she'd felt in a long time. Things were definitely looking up.

Maybe all their bad days were finally behind them.

Chapter Seven

For the next two weeks, Shawn barely had time to breathe. The combination of adapting to her job, looking for a new house, going through all of their belongings, plus all the business of the last part of the school year and getting Lauren ready to leave for her summer job as a camp counselor, took up every minute of her time.

Finding another house was her top priority, though. Unfortunately, all the houses Ann showed her were either not suitable or were priced higher than her budget allowed.

"But Shawn," Ann said after Shawn nixed another house, citing budget restraints, "you can afford this. Actually, you'd qualify for a much larger loan."

"I know. But I don't want to be house poor." Shawn wanted a comfortable margin between her housing costs and her take-home paycheck. She didn't want to be in a position where she would have to tap into her savings if there were any emergency at all…or if she wanted to do something special…like take a vacation.

"Well," Ann said, sighing. "I'm sorry, but there just aren't that many houses in your price range. There's nothing else to show you right now."

Shawn's shoulders sagged. Maybe she and Lauren would have to move into an apartment, the way Rick had. The prospect depressed Shawn. She loved to garden; it was her passion. And Trixie. Trixie needed a yard to run around in. If they were forced to move into an apartment, they might have to find another home for the dog.

"Mom, you've *got* to find something," Lauren said, near tears at the idea they might not be able to keep Trixie. And when Shawn looked at the dog's soft, trusting eyes, she knew she wouldn't have the heart to give her away, either.

But what was she going to *do* if there wasn't a house they could afford?

In the end, Matt saved the day. After she'd cried on his shoulder in an e-mail, he called her the next evening to say there was a house on the next block that had just gone up for sale by owner. "It's small, but it looks like it's been well maintained."

Shawn thanked him and immediately drove over and looked at the outside of the house. Matt was right, it *did* look as if the owners had taken good care of it. A red brick bungalow with a wide front porch and dormer windows on the second floor, it had climbing roses at one corner of the porch and a huge blue spruce tree in the front yard. Shawn could just see that tree all lit up at Christmastime. As Matt had said, there was a sign in front. Mentally crossing her fingers, Shawn parked across the street, took out her cell phone and called the number listed on the sign.

A man with a quavery voice answered. When Shawn explained who she was and that she was interested in the house, then confessed she was sitting in the car across the street, the man, whose name was Franklin— "Benjamin Franklin, my mother was a comedienne," he said—invited her to come over right then. "My wife, Alice, she isn't home right now, but I'll be glad to show you around."

Shawn smiled. She knew, even before seeing Mr. Franklin in person, that he had to be in his eighties. Sure enough, a stooped, white-haired man with a cane walked out onto the porch and watched her cross the street.

"Well, howdy, there, young lady," he said. He had a friendly smile and bright blue eyes.

"Hello, Mr. Franklin. I appreciate you letting me look at the house with so little notice."

"No problem whatsoever. My Alice, she keeps the house spotless, so it's ready for people to see anytime. She'll be mad that she wasn't here, though. But it's Tuesday night, and every Tuesday night for the past thirty-six years, ever since they started having bingo there, she's been down to St. Mary's playing that game with her Altar Society buddies. She usually wins something when she goes, too. I always tell her she shouldn't fool around with such small potatoes. If she's that lucky, we should be going to Las Vegas! Actually, I'm the lucky one, because I got her, and all she ended up with is me. I tell her that all the time, too."

Shawn smothered a smile as he kept talking, telling her all about his Alice and their life together.

"Our only regret is we only had but one child, and she doesn't live close by. Married a career military man, and after he retired, they settled in Arizona. Don't get to see our grandchildren very often," he added sadly, "although the oldest, Celeste, she travels on business a lot, and when she's in our neck of the woods, she always comes by to see us." He smiled. "Do you have any children?"

"I do," Shawn said. "A daughter."

"Well, I imagine you're sick of listening to me talk, so come on, I'll show you around."

The house was perfect. She knew it almost immediately. The downstairs consisted of a living room, a dining room and a kitchen. Both the living room and dining room were small, but the living room had built-in book-cases on either side of a fireplace and the dining room had a charming window seat the complete length of the room, with drawers for storage underneath. The kitchen, though, was surprisingly large and looked as if it had been updated.

"My Alice, she wanted a big eat-in kitchen," Mr. Franklin explained, "for when the family *did* come to visit. We remodeled this one well nigh on twenty-five years ago, I reckon. Tore out the original wall between the old kitchen and the bedroom that used to be over there—" he waved his arm toward the left "—and this is what we ended up with."

Shawn was already mentally placing her big maple table and chairs at one end and thinking how bright the kitchen must be in the mornings, facing east as it did. The paint would have to be changed, though. Currently the walls were painted green, and Shawn was not a green person. Sunny-yellow with red accents. That's what she'd have. She was also pleased to see a gas stove rather than electric.

There was also a small, enclosed back porch. That alone would have been enough to practically sell Shawn on the house, for she could just picture Trixie there in bad weather.

Upstairs were two bedrooms of nearly identical size, one facing the front of the house, the other facing the back, with a huge bathroom containing an old-fashioned claw-foot tub in between. "Just the one bath-room?" she asked, thinking how spoiled she and Lauren were now in their three-bathroom house.

"There's another small bathroom in the basement, which is finished," Mr. Franklin said. "And we put in a shower stall down there." He smiled. "That was for me. So I could shower after working in the yard without tracking dirt upstairs."

"Why are you selling the house, Mr. Franklin?" Shawn asked as they headed downstairs.

He sighed. "As you can see, I have a hard time getting around now. I can't garden much anymore, and the yard's really too much for me. And my Alice, it's getting harder for her to keep the house as clean as she likes it. It's getting so we have to hire people to help us. So we're going to move into that new assisted-living place over on Chestnut Hill."

It was too bad, Shawn thought, for them, at least. But a stroke of good luck for her. If the price was right, that was.

When they reached the basement, Shawn found a large, finished room that could be a game room or a place for Lauren to hang out with her friends, as well as a laundry area, the furnace and a separate fruit cellar.

"I see your wife likes to can," Shawn said, looking at the shelves of canned peaches, tomatoes and pickles.

"Oh, yes. I keep telling Alice we'll never use all this food, but she just keeps on canning, anyway. Says she likes to do it. Truth is, we give most of it away to neighbors and friends."

Shawn knew she should be smart about making an offer on the house and not act too eager, but she loved the place. And when Mr. Franklin told her the price they were asking, she knew the house would not stay on the market long, because it was, if anything, underpriced.

"I'll take it," she said.

"You haven't even seen the garage or the backyard yet."

"I want to see both, but they don't really matter. This house is perfect for me and my daughter." She took out her checkbook. "I'll give you an earnest money check right now."

"We just put the house up for sale yesterday," Mr. Franklin said, obviously bemused. "I don't even have any contracts yet. I was going to go down to the office-supply store tomorrow and get some."

"We can handwrite an agreement," Shawn said. She did not want to take a chance on someone else coming and stealing this house out from under her.

So that's what they did. They sat down at the dining-room table and Shawn wrote out a simple agreement saying she agreed to pay X number of dollars for the house and was giving the Franklins a check for two thousand dollars as an earnest money binder, and that the Franklins agreed to sell her the house pending an inspection and give her possession by the end of June. That meant she would have to stay in a motel for a couple of weeks between vacating her house and moving into this one, or maybe she could stay with Zoe, but that was okay. A little inconvenience was a small price to pay for getting such a great house for such a great price.

After writing Mr. Franklin a check, Shawn told him she'd contact her mortgage company and they'd be in touch, and she said goodbye. After climbing into her car, she impulsively headed around the block and pulled up in front of Matt's house. She figured he deserved to be the first to know about the house, since he was the one responsible for her finding it.

"Shawn!" he said, his eyes lighting up when he answered the door. "What a nice surprise!"

When he smiled at her like that, she got a funny feeling in her stomach. *Stop that. You're just friends, remember?*

"C'mon, in," he said.

Although she was dying to see the inside of his house, she said, "No, I, um, I'd better not. I just stopped by to tell you—"

"Shawn…it won't kill you to come inside for a minute." He held the screened door open.

Her heart thumped as their eyes met. Why did he have to be so darned attractive? "No, Matt, I really can't. Lauren's at the mall and she'll be home soon and—"

Once more he interrupted her, saying, "Do I have to throw you over my shoulder and carry you inside?"

Shawn smiled in spite of herself. "Oh, okay, just for a minute."

She entered a small foyer. To the left was a large archway leading into the living room and to the right was a stairway. "I just wanted to tell you about the house."

"Let's at least sit down." He led her into the living room and gestured toward the fireplace where there was a sofa, two armchairs and a long, narrow coffee table. The sofa was a soft-looking leather in a buttery shade of gold. The armchairs were upholstered in a dark burgundy and the coffee table had a slate top. The only other furnishings were two sets of bookcases, one containing books, the other containing a stereo system. It was a masculine room, yet it was inviting, probably because of the warm colors.

"No TV?" she said, giving him a curious glance.

"Nah, when I'm in here, I'm listening to music and reading. I've got a TV in the den."

"You have a den?"

He grinned. "It's supposed to be the third bedroom, but I turned it into a small TV room. Would you like to see the rest of the house?"

She knew she shouldn't. She should just tell him her news and be on her way, but she was extremely curious. Houses told you so much about people. "I'd love to."

"Before I do, tell me about the house for sale. Did you get to see it?"

Grinning, she said, "Yes. And I loved it! I've already signed a contract to buy it."

"Wow. That was fast."

"I know. But I was afraid someone else would snap it up if I didn't make a quick decision."

"We'll practically be neighbors."

"Yes. In fact, I think his backyard might actually be behind yours."

Matt shook his head. "No, it's two houses up from here."

"I knew it was close."

"So tell me about it." When she'd finished, he said, "It sounds perfect."

"It *is* perfect. And I have you to thank, because that house wouldn't have been on the market for long, not at the price he's asking. I almost feel guilty not offering him more."

"Hey, just consider the price a lucky break. I'm sure the old guy is happy, too. He probably expected you to try to negotiate a lower price. Most people would, you know."

"I know." Shawn could never have been one of those people. She couldn't live with herself if she felt she'd cheated someone. She got up. "I really do need to go, Matt, but I'd love a quick look around at your house."

"As long as you don't look too close." He grinned. "It needs cleaning."

"I promise I won't."

Behind his living room was a small dining room, which currently housed a pool table.

He laughed when he saw her expression. "If I'd had dining-room furniture, this would have gone in the basement. Since I didn't…"

"Very innovative use of space," Shawn said dryly.

From the dining room, they could go directly into the kitchen. It wasn't nearly as large as the one in Shawn's new house—she smiled when she realized she was already thinking of the house as hers—and it was a lot more old-fashioned, with a sink that looked as if it might have been the original one and tile that had seen better days both on the countertops and on the floor.

"If this house were mine, I'd tear out everything in this kitchen," he said, "and start new."

He also had a back porch, but unlike Shawn's house, it wasn't enclosed. One thing the house had that hers didn't, though, was a half bath on the main floor.

When they went upstairs, she saw he had one large bedroom and two tiny ones. One of the small ones was his TV room and the other contained a double bed and dresser and not much else.

"For when I have company," he said.

Because Shawn felt funny about going into his bedroom, she just looked through the doorway, but that quick glance told her Matt was neat. His bed, a king-size, was made up and there were no clothes lying around. "Your mother trained you right," she said, smiling at him.

"You mean because I make my bed?"

"And because you don't leave clothes all over the place." *Unlike Rick,* she thought, who seemed to feel it was part of her job to pick up after him.

There was also a full bathroom upstairs, but it wasn't as large or as nice as Shawn's. She could see, in looking at this house, that the choice she'd made was even better than she'd imagined.

"I'm thinking about buying this place," he said as they walked downstairs.

"Is it for sale?"

"Yeah. When I rented it, the owner said he'd be interested in selling it, maybe next year."

Just before they reached the foyer, Shawn's cell phone rang. Seeing the number, she knew it was Lauren. "Hi," she said.

"Hey, Mom, where are you?"

"I, um, just finished looking at a house. I can't wait to tell you about it, honey. I'll be home in about ten minutes."

"All right. Do I need to walk Trixie?"

"Why don't you wait till I get there and we'll walk her together?"

After disconnecting the call, Shawn said, "That was Lauren."

"I figured."

"She's home from the mall, so I'd better be going."

"Okay. I'll walk you out."

At the car, he said, "When does Lauren leave for camp?"

"Next weekend."

"So I guess this weekend isn't a good one for that movie you owe me."

So he'd remembered. She shook her head. "I'd like to spend this weekend with her."

"I understand, Shawn, but I'm going to hold you to that rain check. How about a week from Saturday? You can choose the movie, and we'll go have pizza or something afterward."

How could she refuse? Especially when she didn't want to. "Okay." She almost said *it's a date,* but stopped herself just in time.

But it *was* a date.

And no amount of rationalizing would ever make it anything else.

When she got to the house, Shawn could hardly contain her excitement. After telling Lauren about the house, she said, "I'm sorry you didn't get to see it before I made my decision, but I was afraid to wait."

"I'm not gonna be here for the move," Lauren said.

"I know, but it can't be helped. Maybe we can go through your things this week before you leave. And you can pack up whatever you're not taking with you."

"Okay."

"I'll go get some boxes from the U-Haul place tomorrow."

"Mom, do you think I could go see the house now?"

"Let me see if Mr. Franklin minds."

When Shawn told the old gentleman how eager Lauren was to see the house, he agreeably said to bring her right over. "My Alice still isn't home, though."

Shawn smiled. Oh, she did like him. Too bad he wasn't going to be a neighbor. She would have enjoyed getting to know him better, as well as "his Alice."

Lauren loved the house, too. She grumbled a bit about sharing the bathroom, but when she saw the finished room in the basement and Shawn told her it would be her domain, she was thrilled and forgot all about the bathroom. "Do you *mean* it, Mom?" she said, eyes shining.

"Yes. It's yours. You can do whatever you want with it, within our budget, of course."

"It'd be so cool if I could have a couch and some chairs down here. And a TV. And a CD player."

"Now Lauren…"

"I know, Mom. But maybe Dad'll give me some money to buy some stuff when I tell him about the room."

Shawn wanted to say *don't hold your breath*, but she was sticking to her resolve not to say anything negative about Rick or Alexandra.

That night, after Lauren had gone to bed, Shawn sat down with her checkbook and calculator. She realized that if she borrowed just a little bit more than she'd planned on, she could afford to let Lauren buy some furniture for the basement room. Maybe she would. After all, Lauren would only be living at home for a few more years. Why not indulge her while she still could? And then, when Lauren eventually got a place of her own, the furniture could go with her. She smiled. Lauren would be so excited. Shawn could hardly wait to tell her.

But before telling Lauren anything more, Shawn knew she had to call Ann. She felt bad about buying a house for sale by the owner, especially since Ann had spent so much time showing her houses, but at least she'd made a nice commission on the sale of *this* house.

Still, Shawn hated having to tell her.

But Ann seemed genuinely happy for Shawn. "Oh, I'm so glad," she said. "I was worried we might not find anything you could afford."

"You're not just saying that, are you?"

"Shawn, you're one of my best friends. I'm happy for you. Honestly."

After hanging up, Shawn thought how lucky she was to have such wonderful friends.

The following morning at breakfast, Lauren chattered nonstop about the house—especially about its "great location." Shawn had an idea she knew why. Lauren must have realized how close they'd be to Matt's house.

Every time Shawn thought about Lauren's obvious crush on her math teacher, she felt guilty about not being entirely honest with her daughter, but it was such a touchy area. Anyway, Matt was probably right. Lauren would be over her schoolgirl crush by the end of the summer, and if Shawn and Matt were still seeing each other then, it would be soon enough to tell Lauren about it.

For the rest of the week, Shawn and Lauren worked every night, and by Friday, they'd pretty much packed everything of Lauren's.

"You'd better hurry and get ready, honey," Shawn said. "Your dad will be here in less than an hour."

Rick and Alexandra were taking Lauren out to dinner for her last night home. Lauren hadn't wanted to go, but Rick had insisted, saying he wanted to talk to her about something before she left for camp.

While she was gone, Shawn indulged herself in a long soak in the tub. Idly, she wondered what it was Rick wanted to discuss with Lauren, but since she had no idea, there was really no sense speculating. Instead, she allowed her mind to dwell on the much more pleasant prospect of her date with Matt the following night.

Afterward, still thinking about Matt, she fixed herself a salad to go with some leftover chicken, then poured a glass of wine and relaxed in front of the TV while she ate.

Later, she gave herself a manicure, and by the time her nails were dry, Lauren was home.

"So what did your dad have to say?" Shawn asked. When Lauren didn't immediately answer, Shawn felt a trickle of alarm. "Is something wrong, honey?"

"No, not really," Lauren said slowly. Her eyes were troubled.

"Lauren, tell me."

Lauren sighed. "Dad and Alexandra…they're going to have a baby."

Shawn felt as if someone had punched her in the stomach. *A baby.* Rick and Alexandra were going to have a baby. She couldn't help but think of all the times she'd been disappointed. Of how much she'd wanted a brother or sister for Lauren. And now Lauren would have one! But Shawn wouldn't be the one to give it to her.

Shawn fought against the flood of emotions that raged inside. The last thing she wanted to do was show Lauren how profoundly this news had affected her. Lauren was the important one now. Drawing on strength she didn't know she had, Shawn managed to say, "Are you okay about this, honey?"

Lauren shrugged. "I guess."

But Shawn could see she *wasn't* okay. Walking over, she put her arms around Lauren and drew her close.

"Think of it this way," she said gently. "You'll have a little brother or sister who will idolize you."

"I know."

Shawn heard the tears in Lauren's voice, and her heart ached for her. *Oh, Rick,* she thought, *you just keep on hurting us, don't you?* She knew the thought was unworthy of her. She knew she shouldn't be envious. But she couldn't help it. She was human. And she'd wanted another child so badly. But this, too, would pass. It was just that the news was such a shock. Then she had another thought. No wonder they'd gotten married so quickly!

Lauren finally pulled away. "I'm okay, Mom." She even managed a shaky smile. "Don't worry about me. And you're right. It'll be neat to have a baby brother or sister."

Shawn had never been prouder of her daughter. Even if she suspected that Lauren wasn't being completely honest.

Chapter Eight

Shawn spent the day sorting and packing and trying not to think about the upcoming evening. So, of course, that's all she *could* think about.

Matt had said he'd pick her up at six-thirty, so at five, she headed for the shower. The hot water helped wash away some of her soreness—packing was hard work—and by the time she'd gotten out and towel dried her hair, she felt refreshed and much less tired.

Since it was going to be a casual evening, she put on a pair of khaki cropped pants, a black tank top and black sandals. She would also take a black sweater along because the theaters tended to be cold. She'd just finished applying her makeup when the doorbell rang.

Frowning, she looked at her watch. It was only six o'clock. It couldn't be Matt already, could it?

It wasn't. It was Rick. A rather scruffy-looking Rick, wearing paint-stained shorts and an old Cleveland Browns T-shirt. He obviously hadn't shaved that day, either. *Well,* she thought nastily, *the bloom has worn off the rose if he's up to his old, sloppy habits.* Immediately, she was ashamed of herself. It wasn't like her to be so vindictive. After all, she no longer cared *what* Rick did. It would be much better to hope that his and Alexandra's relationship worked out so that Lauren wouldn't have to be part of another emotional breakup.

"I came to pick up my stuff," he said.

Still, no matter her good intentions, it irritated Shawn that he thought he could drop by without calling first. But she guessed she should be glad he hadn't just let himself in, since he still had a key.

"You're lucky you caught me home." She didn't even bother to hide her annoyance. "Half an hour later, and I'd have been gone."

"Sorry." But he didn't look sorry. Eyeing her, he said, "You look nice. Going out with the girls?"

That *really* irritated her, that he'd just *assume* she was going out with her girlfriends. That there couldn't possibly be any way she'd have a *date!*

So it gave her great pleasure to say, "No, actually, I have a date."

Something flashed in the depths of his eyes. "Anyone I know?" he said casually.

Shawn wasn't fooled by the offhand question. "I doubt it."

"Try me."

There was definitely something in his blue eyes that told her it bothered him to think of her dating. He probably thought she still cried every night over him. *Think again, buster. You aren't worth more tears.* "Who I date really isn't any of your business, is it, Rick?" she answered coolly.

He seemed taken aback, then simply shrugged and said, "Have it your way, Shawn. I was just trying to be friendly."

Sure you were. "Your things are in the dining room. I packed them up for you."

Although he had already taken a large portion of his belongings, these were things like his skis and hunting and fishing gear and old college yearbooks and mementos that had been stored in the attic, the basement and various closets.

They were dividing the furniture, too, but he had arranged for the movers to deliver his half when they moved her on Tuesday.

It took Rick a while to load the boxes into the back of the pickup truck he'd borrowed. Shawn kept glancing at her watch, half-afraid Matt would show up before Rick finished, and half wanting him to so that Rick could see she not only had a date, but her date was younger than him as well as very good-looking.

It was a few minutes before six-thirty when Rick put the last box in the truck. Shawn decided it was for the best that he and Matt hadn't crossed paths. The last thing she needed would be for Rick to say something to Lauren, either on the phone or in an e-mail, about meeting her mother's date. It would be bad enough if it were just the fact Lauren didn't know Shawn *was* dating, but the added complication of Lauren's crush on Matt made it doubly important that Shawn be the one to break the news.

"What time do you think the movers will get here on Tuesday?" Rick asked.

"They said eight o'clock." Was he hanging around on *purpose?*

"Will you call me when they're about ready to leave here?"

"I told you I would. At the office, right?"

"Or you could just call Alexandra. She'll be at the apartment."

Shawn shook her head. "I'll just call you." Even though she was working on not harboring bitterness toward either one of them, she still wasn't ready to talk to Alexandra. Sometimes she thought she never would be.

He hesitated, then said, "Lauren told you about the baby, didn't she?"

"Yes." Damn. She couldn't help the momentary ache in her heart and hoped her emotions didn't show in her face or her eyes. "Congratulations."

"Thanks." His eyes softened. "Shawn, I'm really sorry about…everything."

She shrugged. "Don't worry about it, Rick. I'm fine, you know."

"Are you? You still seem…I don't know…angry."

"And if I *were,* wouldn't you say I had a right to be?"

He started to answer, then broke off as Matt's Jeep swung into the driveway.

Shawn smiled as Matt, looking satisfyingly handsome and sexy in tight jeans and a black T-shirt, got out and walked toward them.

"Hi," he said, smiling at her, then looking curiously at Rick.

"Hi. Um, Matt, this is Lauren's father, Rick Fletcher. Rick, this is my friend, Matt McFarland." She'd almost said Matt was one of Lauren's teachers, but realized in the nick of time that that would not be wise.

The men did that thing men do. They gave each other the once-over. Shawn was gratified to see that Matt was more than a match for Rick. In fact, if a person was scoring the two men, Matt would be a ten and Rick no more than a seven. Of course, Shawn was prejudiced, but she could see, now that she was more objective about her ex, that Rick was beginning to show his age. If Shawn wasn't mistaken, he'd put on a few pounds, and they didn't look good on him, and wasn't his hair thinning on top?

Before either man could say anything more than hello, Shawn said, "Well, we need to get going. I'll talk to you on Tuesday, Rick."

Not giving him a chance to answer, Shawn turned to Matt. "C'mon in for a minute while I get my purse and put Trixie in her crate."

"It was nice to meet you," Matt said to Rick.

"Yeah, nice to meet you, too," Rick answered, but it was obvious to Shawn that he didn't mean it.

Shawn breathed a sigh of relief when he then climbed into the truck and took off.

"So that's the ex, huh?" Matt said as they walked into the house.

Shawn couldn't tell what he was thinking. "Yes, that's him. He came to pick up the rest of his things."

"I figured. So are you all packed now?"

Shawn laughed. "I wish. I'll be working from sunup till sundown tomorrow."

"I'm free tomorrow. Why don't I come and help?"

"Oh, Matt, you don't have to do that."

"I know I don't have to. I want to."

Shawn smiled. "In that case, you talked me into it. The more hands, the faster things will go. My Wednesday-night group is coming, too, all but Emma."

"Emma's the young one, right?"

"Yes, and she's been accepted in a summer program at Juilliard, so she's gone till the middle of August."

Matt whistled. "Juilliard, huh? She must really be good."

"She's unbelievable, plays both the violin and piano, and she's got a gorgeous soprano voice. At first Zoe was against her studying music. She wanted her to do something that would assure her of a good job when she graduates from college, but music is all that's ever interested Emma."

"Didn't you tell me Zoe is also a singer?"

"Yes. She's got a beautiful alto voice. She's sung in our church choir for years. That's actually how I first met her."

He smiled. "You mean you sing, too?"

"I'm a passable second soprano."

"Modesty. So charming in a woman."

Shawn laughed. "I'm not modest. I'm truthful."

"Honesty. So charming in a woman."

Now she really laughed. "Oh, stop it."

By now she'd collected her purse and gotten Trixie settled, and they headed off to the movie. As before, Shawn had a fun and relaxing evening, even though the undercurrent of sexual attraction between them seemed to grow stronger every moment. She was acutely aware of him sitting next to her, could feel his warmth and smell his aftershave. At times she had a hard time concentrating on the movie because all she could think about was him sitting so close.

She knew Matt felt the attraction, too. She saw it in his eyes every time he looked at her.

I love being looked at this way, she thought as they settled into a booth at Bella Napoli, her favorite pizza place.

By the time they'd eaten their pizza—made on thin crust and dripping with cheese—and drunk a beer apiece and were on their way back to Shawn's house, she knew she could no longer deny that she wanted their relationship to move from friendship to the next level. Maybe she was being foolish. Maybe she'd end up getting hurt. But right now, she didn't care. She hadn't been so strongly attracted to a man in a long, long time.

Acknowledging her desire made her heart pound.

So what if their relationship didn't have a future? Didn't she deserve to take a chance? To grab what she wanted for once in her life?

By the time they got to the house, and he'd walked her to the back door, she'd decided she would subtly let him know she wanted him to kiss her. Just one kiss. That couldn't hurt.

Could it?

He smiled down at her, saying, "I had a wonderful time tonight, Shawn." Then, as if he'd read her mind, he put his hands on her shoulders, drew her close and lowered his lips to hers.

Oh, my, she thought.

The kiss was incredible.

Maybe it was because Shawn hadn't been kissed like this in so long. Or maybe it was because a first kiss from someone you are so strongly attracted to is so special. Whatever the reasons, she felt the kiss sizzle straight through her body all the way to her toes.

Sighing, she melted against him and let him deepen the kiss. She clung to him as her head spun and her knees turned to jelly.

After a long moment, he lifted his head and looked into her eyes. "I want to make love with you, Shawn," he said raggedly.

"I know." Her voice shook. "I want the same."

Cradling her head against his chest, he whispered, "But I'm not...I don't have any protection with me."

"I don't either," she said regretfully.

It pleased her that he was careful. "It's okay, though. The truth is, I'd rather wait until I'm in the new house. This one has too many negative memories."

This time, his kiss was hard and quick. He didn't have to tell her that he didn't trust himself to stay longer, because she felt the same way.

He waited until she'd unlocked the door, then squeezed her hand and said, "I'll see you in the morning."

Inside, Shawn leaned against the door and closed her eyes. As she waited for her heart to slow, she knew she'd have a hard time sleeping tonight.

* * *

Matt smiled all the way home.

Shawn.

She was wonderful.

Even more wonderful than he'd imagined.

Had he known the first time he saw her that she was going to be important to him?

That ex-husband of hers was really stupid to have let her go. Well, his loss was Matt's gain.

Now all Matt had to worry about was not doing something stupid himself.

Matt showed up at the house at nine o'clock Sunday morning, closely followed by Zoe. Ann, Carol and Susan were coming at noon. Stella had also offered to help, but Shawn had told her it wouldn't be necessary, that there were more than enough hands to get everything done.

Shawn knew her girlfriends were avidly curious about Matt. They kept casting speculative glances his way. What would they think if they knew what had happened between her and Matt last night? she wondered.

That kiss.

Every time she thought about it, she had to be sure she didn't look at Matt, because she knew if she did, everyone in the room would be able to guess what she was thinking. Shawn hated that her face was so open and that her emotions were always right out there for everyone to read, but there wasn't much she could do about it.

Zoe, however, seemed to sense that something was different. At one point during the day, when she and Shawn were upstairs and the others were downstairs, she said, "So what's going on with you and The Hunk?"

"What do you mean?" Shawn said, hoping she wasn't blushing.

Zoe looked at her for a long moment. "You know what I mean," she finally said.

Shawn sighed. "Nothing...yet."

"But?"

"But I'm hoping there will be soon."

Zoe regarded her thoughtfully. "Just be careful, okay?"

"Oh, Zoe, of course, I'll be careful."

"I don't just mean using a condom. I mean be careful of your heart."

Shawn was touched. Her voice was soft when she answered, "Don't worry. I will be."

Zoe nodded, but she didn't look convinced. However, she let the subject drop, for which Shawn was extremely grateful.

That night, when the last box was taped shut, and everyone admitted they were hungry, Matt said he'd go pick up a couple of buckets of fried chicken. "Some potato salad and coleslaw and beer, too."

Shawn said okay, but she insisted on paying for everything.

"I'll go with you," Zoe said to Matt.

"You don't have to. Stay and relax."

"No, I want to."

As the two of them walked out the door, Shawn knew Zoe was going to talk to Matt about her. She wasn't sure how she felt about that, but she knew there wasn't anything she could do to prevent it short of lassoing Zoe. And if she did *that,* everyone would know something was going on.

No, best not to make a big deal out of this. Just let Zoe do whatever it was she felt she had to do.

Like I intend to do what I want to do, no matter what Zoe or anyone else has to say about it.

Matt liked Shawn's friends. Especially Zoe, who was the kind of no-nonsense type he respected. You always knew where you were with people like her.

She didn't disappoint him.

They'd no sooner gotten settled into his Jeep and started on their way to the fast-food chicken place when she said, "Shawn's a special person."

He smiled. "Yes, she is."

"I think the world of her."

"I can tell."

"She's been through a lot the past six months."

"I know."

"Do you?"

He glanced over and their eyes met briefly. "Yes, Zoe, I do."

"I hope so. Because I don't want to see her hurt any more than she already has been by that louse of an ex-husband of hers."

"What makes you think *I'll* hurt her?"

"You might not *intend* to, but the situation looks volatile to me."

"In what way?"

Zoe sighed elaborately. "Look, Matt, I think you're a nice guy. I also think you're too smart not to know what I'm talking about. Shawn is vulnerable right now. Among other things, when her ex cheated on her with a woman she had befriended, he crushed her ego. Having you, a young, hot, sexy guy expressing interest in her, is very flattering and is going a long way toward showing her she's still desirable and that there are men out there—young, hot, *sexy* men—who think she's worth pursuing. That's the good part of the situation with you. The bad part is what will happen when you get tired of her and decide you're moving on to a younger woman who doesn't come with baggage."

Matt wasn't sure whether to be amused or annoyed. In answering, he chose his words carefully. "I think it's great Shawn has a friend like you, but what you want from me, I can't give you. I have no idea where my relationship with Shawn is going to end up. I know where

I'd like it to go, but I can't predict the future. I mean, hell, Shawn could decide to move on and break *my* heart!" For a moment, he was afraid Zoe wouldn't appreciate his feeble attempt at humor.

Then she laughed. "Yeah. You're right. I apologize."

"No need to apologize. I admire you for being such a good friend."

By now they'd reached the restaurant, and as they walked inside, Zoe took his arm. She looked up at him and smiled. "I hope things *do* work out with you and Shawn," she said.

He grinned. "That means a lot, coming from you."

"However," she said sternly, "if you *do* break her heart, you'll answer to me. And that's a promise."

The movers finished unloading Shawn's furniture and boxes at five o'clock Tuesday afternoon. Their truck was still in front of the house when Matt's Jeep pulled into her driveway. When he got out, Shawn saw he was carrying a bag of food from a nearby Chinese restaurant.

"How'd you know I was starving?" she said, striving for lightness although just the sight of him had hollowed out her nether regions.

"I figured you'd be too busy to think about food today."

Oh, that smile of his did things to her. Things that should be against the law.

"I did have a bag of potato chips and an apple about eleven this morning."

He grinned. "One vegetable, one fruit, that's not bad."

She laughed. "That's a charitable way to put it—chips as veggie. So what did you bring?"

"Shrimp lo mein, cashew chicken, and wonton soup."

"What?" she said with a mock frown. "No spring rolls?"

"Greedy, aren't you?"

Their gazes met. Shawn's mouth went dry. All she could think about in that moment was the way they'd left each other on Saturday night. Her heart pounded and it took all her willpower to tear her gaze away. *This isn't the time,* she told herself. For all she knew, Zoe and the rest of her girlfriends would be showing up tonight, too.

"C'mon in," she said.

After depositing the food in the kitchen, she gave him a quick tour of the house.

"You did good, Shawn. This is a great house. Great potential."

"I have you to thank."

"All I did was tell you it was for sale."

"Thank goodness you did. Otherwise, it probably wouldn't have lasted on the market a day."

"It was really nice of the Franklins to let you move in earlier, too."

"Yes, it was. Otherwise, I'd've had to put my stuff in storage and I'd be in a motel tonight."

They headed back to the kitchen where he unpacked and opened the food and Shawn rooted around until she found the box she'd labeled OPEN FIRST. Slitting the tape, she delved inside and retrieved a couple of plates and a bag of utensils.

"No napkins, I'm afraid," she said ruefully.

"I brought some," he said. "Chopsticks, too."

"You can eat with *chopsticks?*"

"It's easy. I'll teach you, if you want."

"You're definitely a man of many talents…." Realizing what she'd said could be construed as a double entendre, Shawn blushed. That was the trouble with sex. Once you thought about it with a certain person, it was impossible to be around that person *without* thinking about it.

"After we eat," he said, "I'll help you get your appliances hooked up and working."

"That'd be great," Shawn said around a mouthful of cashew chicken.

"I'm trying to make myself indispensable."

"You're doing a good job."

Their gazes locked.

She swallowed.

"I wish," he began.

"Me, too," she murmured. "But not tonight."

"I know."

It was a darned good thing they'd decided it wasn't the night to make good on their promise, for they'd barely finished their dinner when the doorbell rang. Zoe, Carol and Susan stood on the doorstep.

"Ann had an appointment to list a house," Carol said, "or she'd be here, too." Carol was carrying a sack of hamburgers. "Did you eat?"

"Just finished."

"Oh, well, more for us," Carol said.

It was then the women noticed Matt, who was standing in the kitchen doorway.

"Should we go? Maybe you want to be alone," Susan said in a stage whisper.

"Don't be silly!" Shawn said. Now she *knew* she was blushing.

With all the help she had, Shawn not only got her appliances hooked up and working, she got her bed put together, her linens and towels unpacked, her kitchen cabinets wiped out, and most of her kitchen equipment unpacked and put away. Zoe even unpacked her pantry items and found the coffee so that Shawn would have coffee in the morning.

At ten o'clock, Shawn insisted they all go home. "I can't thank you enough for what you've done, but you've all got to work tomorrow."

"Not me," Matt said. "I can stay longer."

Shawn's heart skipped. She couldn't meet his eyes, nor could she look at her friends. Yet somehow she managed to hug each woman goodbye. Zoe was last. As they hugged, Zoe whispered in Shawn's ear, "Remember, be careful."

Finally they were gone.

Shawn turned. Her gaze slowly met Matt's. He didn't smile or say anything. He simply looked at her. But she saw the question in his eyes.

She wanted to say yes.

But… "I'm so sweaty and dirty," she finally said.

"So am I." He walked forward. When he was standing directly in front of her, he tipped her chin up and lightly, oh, so lightly, kissed her mouth, letting his tongue linger.

Shawn shuddered as his tongue traced the inside of her lips and she felt a deep pull inside.

"There's a nice, big tub upstairs," he murmured against her mouth. "I'll bet we could both fit inside."

Then he kissed her again, and this time it wasn't gentle or light. This time it was passionate and deep and demanding. When he finally let her up for air, Shawn would have agreed to anything, anything at all, if it meant he'd kiss her again, if it meant he'd make love to her. Because right then, nothing else in the world mattered. Not the future. Not the past. Only this moment and this man and the promise in his eyes.

In unspoken agreement, they locked the doors and turned out the lights downstairs. Then, hand in hand, they walked upstairs.

"I'll fill the tub," he said.

Shawn nodded. "There's bubble bath."

He smiled. "I know. I saw it before."

"While you do that, I want to get something."

Giving her a quick, hard kiss, he muttered, "Don't be too long."

Shawn moved in a daze toward the linen closet where she'd earlier stored a box of votive candles and several books of matches that had been packed in with her towels. She also wanted her clock radio so they could have music.

When she entered the bathroom, Matt had stripped down to his jeans, and the sight of his muscled chest made her breathing accelerate.

Suddenly shy, she didn't meet his eyes as she set the radio on the countertop and plugged it in. Within moments, she'd found the station she wanted—one that played love songs from ten till midnight every night. With the music playing softly, she started placing the votive candles around the room, lighting each one as she went.

When she finished, she turned out the light. Then, in the flickering candlelight, while Matt watched, she took a deep breath for courage, and began to remove her clothes.

Matt couldn't have moved if his life depended on it. He could only watch. And marvel...that this woman, this sexy, beautiful woman, wanted him the way he wanted her.

How'd I ever get so lucky?

God, she was gorgeous.

He knew she didn't think so, but she was. He liked everything about her, from her mass of blond curls to her polished pink toenails, and everything in between.

When her T-shirt and jeans were gone and she stood before him clad only in flesh-colored bikini panties and a matching bra, he sucked in his breath. She had a great body. It wasn't perfect, but it was damn near.

For a long moment, he just looked. Then he finally found his voice. "You're beautiful," he said softly.

"I'm not."

"Yes, you are."

She licked her lips. "Um, do you want to get in?"

He smiled. And unzipped his jeans. Then, never taking his eyes from hers, he pushed down his briefs and stepped out of them.

He heard her swift intake of breath as her eyes lowered and she saw how aroused he was. Then, swallowing, she unhooked her bra. Her hands were trembling, he saw, but she managed to take the bra off.

Now it was his turn to suck in a breath. Her breasts, while not large, were perfect. Suddenly, he couldn't wait another second. He reached for her and pulled her roughly into his arms. They kissed hungrily, and the feel of her softness against him was almost more than he could bear.

Slow down, he told himself. He wanted this to be good for her, a home run with the bases loaded. But at this rate, he wasn't even going to get to first base.

Forcing himself to take a deep breath, he looked down into her eyes. "Let's get these off you, too, then we'll get in, okay?"

"Okay."

As he slid her panties down, revealing a soft nest of blond hair, he couldn't resist cupping her bottom and putting his mouth against her. He slid his tongue inside for one delicious moment, moving it up and down while she moaned softly.

Letting her panties drop, he picked her up and put her into the hot water. Swiftly, he climbed in behind her. Pulling her tight against him, he settled her bottom against himself and reached for the soap.

Shawn was sure she'd died and gone to heaven. Nothing had ever felt this wonderful. Nothing.

Matt soaped her everywhere, letting his hands act as a washcloth. All the while, she could feel his rock-hard penis against her bottom. When he slid his fingers inside her, probing until he found the exact spot that craved his touch, she gasped.

"Easy," he whispered, kissing her neck and then her ear as he continued stroking with his soapy hands.

But Shawn was too far gone. She shuddered as he brought her to a climax that was almost painful in its intensity. When her body finally calmed, she wanted to do the same for him, but he simply kissed her and said, "This time let's go someplace that's more comfortable."

Five minutes later, clean and dried and wrapped in towels, they headed for Shawn's bed.

Without embarrassment, he reached for a condom, then naked, they lay twined together on top of Shawn's crisp, cool sheets. Now they kissed. Over and over again. When Shawn reached for him, he groaned. Moments later, saying he couldn't wait much longer, he entered her, slowly at first, then thrusting hard.

"Yes, yes," Shawn said as he drove deep inside. She wrapped her legs around him and matched her moves to his. *Matt,* she thought. *Matt.* She was going to have another orgasm, she could feel it coming, and just as the first ripple of pleasure began, he cried out and his body shuddered in release.

Afterward, when he would have pulled out, she wouldn't let him. She loved feeling him inside her. She loved the weight of him on top of her.

She loved *him.*

The realization scared her…and yet it thrilled her, too.

They had a lot of problems, she knew that. Lauren, Shawn's inability to get pregnant, the age difference.

But right then, none of those things mattered.

Shawn smiled.

Like Scarlett O'Hara, she wouldn't think about them today. She'd think about them tomorrow.

Chapter Nine

Lauren wasn't enjoying her summer as much as she had the previous year. She missed Matt so much. It was awful to be so far away from him. If only she could talk to him or even e-mail him, but she didn't dare call him. What could she possibly say? And she didn't know his e-mail address except for the one at school, which he wouldn't be checking over the summer.

She sighed. Ever since meeting Matt, no one else compared. Last year she'd had a huge crush on Doug Fields, one of the other counselors. She'd thought he was so cool. But this year he seemed so immature…a boy…whereas Matt was a man.

Matt…

"Hey, Lauren! Wait up!"

Jerked out of her daydream, Lauren looked up. Coming toward her was Doug Fields, almost as if he'd known she had been thinking about him. "Oh, hi, Doug," she said without much enthusiasm.

He grinned at her. "I was looking for you. You coming to the party down at the lake tonight?"

After the campers were asleep, a bunch of the counselors were getting together to swim and listen to music and dance.

The question made her uncomfortable because she knew why he was asking. "Yeah, I guess."

"Want me to come by and get you?"

"No, that's okay. I'm not sure where I'll be."

"Well, you've got your cell, don't you?"

"Yes, but, I think it would be better if we both just go when we're ready. You might want to go earlier than me."

He shrugged. "Sure, okay. It'll be fun. Jim said he'd get us some hot dogs and stuff." Jim Bruner was a high-school basketball coach who was in charge of the sports program at the camp this year.

"Yeah, I heard."

"He said we had to be in our cabins by midnight, though."

That suited Lauren. She didn't even want to go to the dumb party.

"So I guess I'll see you there, then."

"Yeah, see you."

With a wave, he walked off in the direction of the tennis courts, where she knew he was teaching a class.

Now Lauren felt bad. Doug *was* nice. She *did* like him. If he'd paid attention to her like this last year, she would have been thrilled. But things were different now. This year she only thought of him as a friend.

Lauren sighed again. She didn't want to hurt Doug's feelings, but she didn't want to give him the wrong idea, either. She wished there was a way to tell him nicely that she was interested in someone else, but he hadn't really given her an opening, and she couldn't just blurt it out.

Crap. Why did life have to be so complicated sometimes? And why couldn't boys like you when you liked *them?* Sometimes it seemed as if they only *really* liked you when you played hard to get.

Is that what Doug thought? That she was playing hard to get?

Although Lauren had been heading toward the cabin she shared with three other counselors, she now reversed direction and took the path leading to the library and adjoining computer center. At this time of the afternoon, when all the campers were either in class or down at the lake, she ought to find a free computer.

She was in luck. Only one of the six available computers was in use. Settling at one, she went to the Webmail program that would allow her to access her e-mail account. She had three new e-mails, one from her mother, one from Heather and one from her dad.

After reading them, she replied to her mother first.

Hi, Mom, she wrote, Sounds like you're really on top of the unpacking. Just don't do anything in my room or down in the basement, okay? Remember, you promised I could fix both of them up any way I wanted. I just got e-mail from Dad, and he said he'll give me a thousand dollars toward some new furniture. That ought to be enough for a couch and TV for the basement, and with what's left, maybe we could try some of the garage sales or that big flea market. What do you think?

Lauren continued, giving her mother a rundown of what had happened at camp since she'd arrived the week before, although she omitted all mention of Doug. Then, at the end, she wrote, You know, I think our new house is around the corner from where my math teacher, Mr. McFarland, lives. If you see him, tell him I said hi.

Lauren looked at what she'd written. It wasn't what she wanted to say at all, but it was the best she could come up with. Maybe, if she was lucky, her mom had already run into Matt and would write her back and tell her about it. Maybe he'd even asked about her.

She wished she could think of a reason to ask her mother to get his e-mail address, but she couldn't.

She signed the e-mail and sent it, then answered

Heather and her dad. She didn't say anything about Doug to Heather, either, because of course she couldn't explain why she wasn't interested, so why bring it up at all?

When she was finished with her e-mails, she finally went to her cabin where she managed to snag a nap—and dreamed about Matt—before it was time to help in the crafts class. She enjoyed crafts class. She always had a good time working with the kids. That day, they learned how to weave a basket, which was not only fun, but kept her mind occupied so she didn't think about Matt or Doug. When class was over, it was time for dinner.

After dinner, there was a special magic show for the kids, then Lauren and the other counselors worked with their individual groups until it was time to herd everyone off to their cabins and bed.

It was nine-thirty before Lauren was free to walk down to the lake. When she got there, several of the boys had already built a fire. Some of the kids had even begun cooking hot dogs and a few were toasting marshmallows.

Someone else had brought a boom box and rap music blared. Lauren wasn't crazy about rap, but she didn't intend to stay, anyway, so it didn't matter. Since she was trying to lose a few pounds this summer—if she were thinner, she'd look older—she ignored the food and headed to the cooler where she grabbed a diet root beer, then walked over to where Mimi DesPlaines was sitting on a big rock. Mimi was new this year, and Lauren had liked her immediately.

"Hey," she said.

"Hey," Mimi said, moving over to make room for Lauren.

For a while, they just sat quietly watching the others. Soon there were several dozen kids there.

"There's Doug," Mimi said. "He's looking for you."

"No, he's not," Lauren said. But she could see him scanning the group. She hurriedly looked away. The last thing she wanted was for him to think she was looking for *him*.

"You know he likes you, Lauren."

Lauren heaved a sigh.

"He's cute."

"Yeah, I know." *But he's not Matt.*

"Oh, there's Trey."

Lauren smiled. Mimi had a big-time crush on Trey Harden, one of the lifeguards. And it looked like he felt the same way, for the moment he spied her, his whole face broke into a smile and he headed in their direction. Unfortunately, Doug was right behind him.

Lauren swore under her breath.

"Hi, Mimi. Hi, Lauren," Trey said, but he only had eyes for Mimi. "Wanna dance?"

She stood. "Sure."

"So you made it," Doug said, sitting down next to Lauren.

"Yeah." Lauren drank some of her root beer.

"I'd ask you to dance but I don't like this crap," Doug said.

"You don't?"

Doug shook his head.

"What kind of music *do* you like?" Even though Lauren didn't want to encourage him, she was curious. Besides, they had to talk about *something*.

"Promise you won't laugh."

"I won't laugh."

"I like show tunes."

Lauren couldn't believe it. "You *do?*" She totally *loved* show tunes. She and her mom loved to go into Columbus and see Broadway shows at the Ohio Theater. They hadn't gone much lately because of the divorce and money and everything, but her mom had told her just last week that they'd go for her birthday in September. In fact, she'd already ordered tickets.

"Do you think I'm stupid?" he asked.

"No! I like show tunes, too."

"You do?"

"Yes, totally. My favorite show is *Chicago*. That music is awesome."

"Yeah! Did you see the movie?"

"Only about a dozen times."

He grinned. "Me, too. I bought the DVD. Which one is your favorite song?"

"'All That Jazz.'"

"Mine's 'Mr. Cellophane.'"

"I like that one, too. A lot."

"I saw *Chicago* on Broadway," Doug said.

Lauren had never been to New York. She wanted to go in the worst way, but so far, it hadn't worked out. Maybe when she and Matt…

"What's wrong?" Doug asked.

"Nothing."

"You didn't think I was bragging?"

Lauren shook her head. "No, of course not. I—I just thought of something…." She stood. "Listen, Doug, I'm going to head back to my cabin. My stomach's a little upset."

"Oh, I'm sorry." He stood, too. "I'll walk you back."

"No, you don't have to do that. I don't want you to miss the party."

"You're the only reason I came, anyway."

Oh, great. Now what could she say?

"C'mon," he said. "Let's go."

What else could she do? She had to let him come with her. But her mind was working overtime trying to figure out what she'd say if he tried to kiss her goodnight.

If he does, I'll just tell him the truth.

Her heart skidded at the thought, because even though she wanted to discourage Doug, she hated hurting anyone's feelings, especially somebody as nice as he was.

It took a while to reach the cabin where Lauren was staying because it was located at the top of a hill almost at the farthest end of the camp. When they got there, Lauren hurriedly said, "Thanks, Doug. See you tomorrow."

He put his hand on her arm. "Lauren, wait…."

They were standing in a pool of lamp light, and she could see from the expression on his face that he wanted to kiss her.

Lauren swallowed. "Doug…I-I'm sorry. I really like you as a friend, but there's this guy at home and…well…"

"Oh. I didn't think you were going with anyone."

"He's older."

He frowned. "Older? Like what? A senior?"

Oh, crap. Why hadn't she just said she was going with someone and left it at that? "Yeah, a senior."

"Oh."

"I'm sorry."

He shrugged. "Hope you feel better."

It was obvious to Lauren that he was trying to pretend he didn't care about what she'd said, but she knew he did. But it was better to tell him than to have to keep dodging him the rest of the summer.

Because no matter how nice Doug was, he wasn't Matt.

The end of summer couldn't come fast enough.

Shawn hated to admit it, even to herself, but she was enjoying being on her own this summer. It was the first time in many years that she had no one to worry about or to answer to. Her time was her own and it was a delicious feeling.

Some days she felt guilty because down deep she was sure a good mother would be missing her daughter. But for the most part, she realized it was probably good for both of them to have this time apart.

She loved fixing up the new house. She loved not having to cook if she didn't want to. But most of all, she loved being with Matt. It was pure heaven to be able to have him come to the house in the evening, to eat take-out Chinese or hamburgers, then to go upstairs to the bedroom and make love slowly, without worrying about Lauren.

Shawn and Matt made love all the time.

In Shawn's bed. In the tub. In Matt's bed. And in his shower. Shawn blushed every time she thought about making love standing up with hot water beating down upon them. It had been incredible. She'd felt wanton and sexy and not like herself at all. In fact, most days she didn't recognize herself. Who *was* this woman who thought about sex all the time?

She had never thought of herself as a particularly sexual person, but with Matt, she was shameless. She woke up wanting him and went to bed wanting him. And if she hadn't been spending her days in an office, she'd have wanted him then, too.

When she confessed all this to her friends during one

of their Wednesday-night dinners early in July, saying she was afraid there was something wrong with her, they just laughed.

"There's nothing wrong with a healthy sexual appetite, Shawn," Carol said. Her eyes were wistful. "I remember when I felt that way."

"Yeah," Susan agreed. "There's nothing like those first delirious months after falling in love."

Zoe nodded ruefully. "Shoot, Shawn, we're all envious. I know I haven't felt that way about a man in a long time."

As always, when Zoe made any reference to her love life, Shawn wondered what Zoe's story was. As close as the two of them had become, Zoe had never confided anything about her past—especially where it concerned Emma. Once, when the two of them had been alone, she'd told Shawn she didn't want to talk about it. She'd said she had been very young and had made a mistake.

"Not that I consider Emma a mistake," she'd hurried to clarify. "She's the best thing that ever happened to me. I mean, in the man I picked."

Shawn wondered if Emma's father had been married and that's why Zoe wouldn't talk about him. But she'd never asked. Zoe was entitled to her privacy. If she ever wanted to share, fine. Otherwise, Shawn would respect the boundaries Zoe had established.

But she did wish Zoe could find her own Matt. She

was so attractive and such a great person. But first she'd have to let down the barriers she'd erected, for she would only let a man get so close and no closer.

"It's more than loving sex with Matt," Shawn confessed later, as she and Zoe were driving home. "I—I think I'm in love with him."

Zoe raised her eyebrows.

"You don't approve, do you?"

"Does it matter what I think?"

"Of course it matters. You're my best friend."

"Shawn…" Zoe sighed. "I think Matt is a great guy. And if you love him, and he loves you, I'm happy for you. I just—"

"What?"

"Well, this has all happened so fast. I just want you to be sure."

Shawn nodded. It *had* happened fast. Maybe that's why she still had some doubts. Had it happened *too* fast? Was what she felt for Matt really love? The kind that would last forever? She was no longer sure she was a good judge of anything. When she'd married Rick she'd thought *theirs* was a love that would last forever, and she'd been wrong. So what made her think she knew any better now?

"Has he told you he loves *you?*" Zoe asked.

"No," Shawn said softly. A couple of times, she'd thought he was going to, but he hadn't.

"Hmm," Zoe said.

"Do…do you think he does?" Oh, God. She sounded so damned *needy.* "I mean, you talked to him. I know you did."

"Yes, I talked to him. And I told him if he hurt you, he'd have to answer to me."

"Zoe! You didn't!" But Shawn was touched.

Zoe laughed ruefully. "I did. And I meant it, too. But in answer to your question, I do think he cares for you. Whether it's love and whether it'll lead to a permanent commitment, I don't know. If that's what you want, I hope it does, Shawn. But if I were you, I'd think long and hard before committing to anyone right now. I think you're still too vulnerable. I think you need to let more time go by to make sure this thing with Matt is real… and not just infatuation…or the thrill of being wanted by a sexy, young guy."

"I hope I'm not that shallow."

"I didn't say you were. Like Carol said earlier, there's nothing wrong with a healthy sexual appetite. I'd go further and say there's nothing wrong with enjoying being wanted. Just so long as you don't confuse those feelings—if that's what you're really feeling—with love."

That night Shawn couldn't sleep. She kept thinking about what Zoe had said.

Was she in love with Matt?

More to the point, was he in love with her?

And if he was, could they build a long-term relationship? Or were their differences too great to surmount?

Those questions would have to be answered…and soon. Because in just three more weeks, Lauren would be home again.

And then what?

one another? Or were they in love, moving toward a permanent, committed relationship?

Shawn wished Matt would bring up the subject, but so far, he hadn't. That night, she knew she couldn't wait any longer. She would have to come right out and ask him what he was thinking. It scared her, because what if she'd read the signals wrong? She thought about how he'd never said he loved her. What if he didn't? What would she do?

They went to a movie at the local theater that night, and she worried her way through it. Afterward, they walked back to her house. They were standing outside, kissing in the moonlight filtering through the screens of the enclosed back porch, when he suddenly sighed and buried his face in her hair.

"Shawn," he whispered. "You know how I feel about you, don't you?"

"I…" What could she say? She *thought* she did, but what if she was wrong?

"I love you," he murmured. "I love you more than I thought I could ever love anyone. I want us to be together forever."

Her heart sang; her entire being filled with joy. "Oh, Matt, I love you, too," she cried. "And that's what I want."

This time when they kissed, she knew they were making a promise to one another.

"After Lauren comes home and gets settled in, we'll talk to her together, okay?" Matt said later, after they'd made love and were lying wrapped in each other's arms.

"I don't know if that's a good idea," Shawn said slowly. "Maybe I should prepare her first. At least tell her I've been seeing you over the summer."

"If you want to do it that way, it's okay with me. I just thought it might be easier to tell her together."

"I'm not sure it would be easier for her." Shawn figured she'd wait and see how Lauren acted when she came home. Shawn could casually bring Matt's name into a conversation, and she was pretty sure she could tell by Lauren's reaction whether she was still harboring that crush on him.

If not, no problem.

But if she *were,* then Shawn would have to tread very carefully to avoid hurting her daughter.

Shawn refused to even think about what she'd do if Lauren *didn't* come around.

Rick said he'd take the day off and go pick up Lauren at camp. Shawn was grateful. She hadn't accumulated much vacation time and, although she knew Stella would probably let her have a personal day, she didn't want to ask for it. Although she'd only worked at the firm less than four months, she could see how swamped Stella was most of the time. In fact, the week before she'd said she thought it was time to look for an associate as well as bigger office space.

"I think we also need a paralegal as well as some help for you," she told Shawn.

It pleased Shawn that Stella realized how hard she'd been working and that she really *did* need help. She was so lucky to work for someone as considerate as Stella, and she knew it. She'd certainly heard horror stories from Zoe and Carol and Susan.

So she didn't want to push her luck by asking for time off unless it was an emergency.

The day of Lauren's homecoming dawned hot and humid—a typical August day in central Ohio. Even the squirrels seemed sluggish this morning, Shawn thought as she drank her coffee and gazed out the kitchen window. Instead of their normal scampering and chasing each other, they were mostly sitting on the branches of the biggest maple tree, doing nothing.

Taking her cue from them, Shawn had dressed in her lightest-weight sleeveless dress, although she was taking along a cardigan sweater because the air-conditioned office could get mighty cold.

All morning she kept looking at the clock. She knew Rick had planned to leave his place at seven and figured he'd arrive at the camp by ten. If he and Lauren got away soon after, she should be home by one. If they stopped for lunch—which they probably would—then she'd be home by two.

Just as Shawn had thought, Lauren called at a little after two to say she was home. "I love the house, Mom," she bubbled. "I've been looking at everything, and it looks great. I can't wait to start buying furniture for the basement room and to start painting and fixing up my bedroom. Maybe I could even get some new curtains."

"We'll look for furniture this weekend," Shawn said. "Curtains, too." She smiled. Her heart felt so full. Lauren was her baby, and she couldn't wait to see her. Despite her misgivings about how Lauren would take the news of Shawn's involvement with Matt, it was good to have her daughter home again. "I'll be there about five-thirty," she said before hanging up. "I'll bring a pizza with me."

"From Bella Napoli?"

"Where else?"

"Get extra cheese, okay?"

"You got it."

Shawn was smiling when they hung up.

Lauren decided unpacking could wait. Right now, there was something much more important to do. After playing with Trixie for a while, she hurriedly washed up, changed into clean white shorts and a pink halter top that showed off her tan, slipped her feet into flip-flops, then took her bike out of the garage and pedaled around the block.

Matt, Matt, Matt.

She wasn't sure what she'd do when she got to Matt's house. It wasn't like she could just go up to the door and knock.

Still, she couldn't resist at least *seeing* the house.

And if he should happen to be outside, she had a perfectly legitimate reason to be biking around the neighborhood, because now it was *her* neighborhood, too.

Oh, she was so happy, she could have hugged herself!

As she approached his house, she couldn't believe her luck, for he *was* outside, cutting his grass. In the few minutes before he saw her, too, she had a chance to study him.

Her heart skidded. He looked wonderful. He wore cutoffs and sneakers and no shirt. His muscles rippled as he worked, and his skin glistened with sweat under the hot sun. He was tanned, too, all over.

Oh, God, he was gorgeous.

She wondered if he'd spent a lot of time swimming this summer, or maybe he'd just gotten his tan running. Her dad got brown every summer just by being on the golf course.

Lauren's heart was beating like crazy as she braked to a stop in front of Matt's house. She grinned and waved when he turned around and noticed her. He stopped mowing, mopped his face with a small towel he'd tucked into his waistband, then headed toward her.

"Hi, Lauren." He smiled.

"Hi, Ma—Mr. McFarland."

"Back from camp, huh?"

He'd remembered! Lauren was thrilled. If he'd remembered, that meant he'd thought about her this summer. "I just got home an hour ago," she said.

"And you're out on your bike already?"

I wanted to see you. The thought was so strong, for a moment Lauren thought she'd spoken it out loud. "I wanted to see the neighborhood."

"So how do you like your new house?"

"I love it. There's this room in the basement that I'm going to be fixing up for myself. A place to entertain my friends." *Maybe someday you'll be down there with me.*

"That sounds nice."

Lauren looked past him. "Did you buy this house?"

"Not yet." He smiled. "I'm still trying to decide if I want to."

"It looks nice from the outside." She wished he'd invite her inside.

"It needs work, but I like it."

Lauren nodded. She thought about saying she was thirsty, but decided not to. If he didn't offer her a drink, she'd be embarrassed.

"Well, I'd better get back to work," he said. "I still have the backyard to do."

"Oh, okay. Well, it was nice seeing you. Guess I'll see you in school in two weeks."

He nodded. "Enjoy the rest of your summer." Giving her another smile, he walked back to his lawn mower.

Lauren rode away. She was dying to know if he was watching her, but she didn't dare look back.

Even though he hadn't invited her to see the house, her heart was singing. Just the fact he'd remembered she was working at camp this summer was enough to tell her what she needed to know. The rest would follow.

All she had to do was be patient.

The moment Lauren was out of sight, Matt abandoned the lawn and went inside. Picking up his cell phone, he punched in the code for Shawn's office.

"Stella Vogel's office."

"Shawn?"

"Oh, hi, Matt."

"Shawn, I have to talk to you. Can you meet me after work?"

"I can't tonight, Matt. Lauren's home, and I told her I'd be there no later than five-thirty."

"Yes, I know. She came by here."

"She came by your *house?*"

"Yes. On her bike. She pretended she was just looking around the neighborhood, but I could tell just from the way she acted, that she'd come to see me." He thought about the way she'd hinted for an invitation to see the house. She still had a crush on him, that was clear.

"Oh, dear." Shawn's sigh was audible. "Matt, we're going to have to be very careful. I don't want to hurt Lauren. She's been hurt enough. And now, with the new baby coming, she's particularly vulnerable...."

"But you *are* going to tell her about us?"

"Yes, but maybe not tonight. Let's talk tomorrow and decide how best to do it, okay?"

Matt guessed that was reasonable. "Okay." His voice softened. "Remember, Shawn, we're in this together."

"I know."

He hoped she *did* know. If he could change anything about his and Shawn's relationship, it would be her attitude toward anything concerning Lauren. He knew she didn't purposely mean to exclude him, but sometimes she acted as if a problem with Lauren was strictly *her* problem. Matt wished he could make her understand that anything affecting her and her life affected him, too.

You're too impatient, Matt.

The voice inside sounded suspiciously like his sister Cathy who had been telling him this very thing for years.

Maybe he *was* too impatient, expecting too much from Shawn too soon. After all, their relationship was still in the beginning stages.

He resolved to be more understanding and to give Shawn as much time as she needed.

What really mattered was that ultimately they would be together.

Lauren had intended to go straight home, but she decided the unpacking could wait until the next day. She was too keyed up to go home.

Besides, she was dying to know all the gossip. Heather wasn't exactly the best correspondent. Her e-mails were mostly about herself and how horrible her summer was and how her mother drove her crazy and how she was totally in love with Colin Finley, blah blah blah.

Lauren rolled her eyes, remembering. Until this summer she hadn't realized how self-centered Heather was. Well, maybe if Lauren went down to Burger Barn, she'd see some of the other kids and she'd get the scoop on what had been happening around here the past two months.

When Lauren walked into the popular high-school hangout, she didn't see any of her crowd, but she did see Annie Campbell, who was in her karate class.

After buying herself a Coke and some French fries, Lauren walked over to the table where Annie was sitting reading and sipping a Coke. "Hi, Annie."

Annie looked up and her glasses slid down on her nose. "Oh. Hi, Lauren."

"Care if I sit down?"

"No."

"You waiting for someone?"

"Just my mom, but she won't be here for another thirty minutes, at least." Annie smiled and put a bookmark in her book, then set it aside. "We're going to go shopping for school clothes."

Lauren almost said *you want your mom along when you pick out clothes?* but thought better of it. Annie was a little bit of a nerd in some ways, but she was nice. Lauren didn't want to hurt her feelings.

"I haven't seen you much this summer," Annie said. She took another sip of her drink.

Lauren explained about being away at camp.

"That sounds like fun."

Lauren grinned. "It was, but I'm glad to be home."

For the next twenty minutes, they talked about school and some of the other kids. Annie told her who'd broken up and who had a new boyfriend. Lauren was laughing and thinking that Annie really was pretty nice. She was getting ready to suggest maybe they could hang out this weekend when Annie said, "Hey, I didn't know your mom and Mr. McFarland had hooked up."

Lauren froze. "What?"

Annie, totally oblivious to Lauren's shock, said, "I was in Columbus last Saturday night with my cousin. We were down on Front Street, and I saw your mom and Mr. McFarland coming out of Ludlow's." Her eyes sparkled with excitement. "They were holding hands and laughing, and he stopped and kissed her, right there on the street! Man, you could see they were hot for each other. He's so cute, I can see why she likes him."

"It—it must not have been my mom."

"Oh, it was her, all right," Annie said. "I know your mom."

Lauren's heart raced. She couldn't believe it. Stricken, she didn't even try to pretend she wasn't upset.

Blurting out, "I—I have to go," she jumped up and practically flew out of the restaurant.

She pedaled home furiously, tears streaming down her face. Her mother and Matt? Together? Kissing? It couldn't be true, could it?

Oh, God. Oh, God.

When she got to the house, she jumped off her bike, letting it crash onto the driveway. She blindly ran inside. Trixie, who'd been on the back porch, followed her in, barking happily. Sobbing, Lauren fell to the floor, burying her face in the dog's fur. Trixie lapped at her face.

No, no, no, Lauren cried inside. It couldn't be true. Annie had to be mistaken. She'd just *thought* she'd seen Lauren's mother with Matt. It had to have been someone else. Someone who *looked* like her mother and Matt. Her mother wasn't even *dating* anyone. If she had been, she would have told Lauren. Wouldn't she?

On and on her mind raced. When her mother came home, she'd clear this up. It was stupid of Lauren to get so upset. Totally stupid.

Telling herself to calm down, she got up off the floor and walked slowly upstairs to her bedroom. It was only four o'clock. It would be at least an hour and a half before her mother came home. *I should do something. The time will go faster if I do.*

But she didn't have the energy or the enthusiasm to do anything other than throw herself across her bed and stare at the ceiling. Her mind whirled with pictures of her mother and Matt.

Could what Annie had told her be true?

And if it was true, did that mean her mom had been having *sex* with Matt?

Lauren swallowed. *I can't stand it. I'll run away if it's true. It can't be true. She wouldn't do that to me.*

Finally the clock read five o'clock, then five-fifteen. Lauren got up, washed her face, combed her hair and walked downstairs. She sat at the kitchen table to wait.

At five-thirty, Lauren heard her mom's car pull into the driveway. She heard the thunk of the car door, then a scraping sound. She realized her mom was picking up her bike and putting it into the garage. Lauren would have felt guilty about leaving the bike lying on the driveway except she was still too upset.

When her mom walked into the kitchen, there was a huge smile on her face. Lauren's heart twisted.

"Oh, sweetie, I'm so glad to see you!" her mom exclaimed, putting the pizza box on the counter and rushing over to put her arms around Lauren.

Lauren allowed the embrace, but she didn't return it.

Drawing back, her mom frowned and searched Lauren's face. "What's wrong, honey?"

Holding herself as still as she could so she wouldn't fall apart, Lauren said, "Is it true?"

"Is *what* true?" Her mom's green eyes were bewildered.

"Annie Campbell told me she saw you and Matt in Columbus last Saturday night. She said you were holding hands. She said he *kissed* you, right there on Front Street, in front of all kinds of people. Is that true?"

Her mother stared at her.

In that moment when their eyes locked, Lauren saw the truth in the depths of her mother's. Lauren's heart was beating so hard, she was afraid it would just pop right out of her chest, and her head felt as if it were going to burst, too.

"Honey, I was going to tell you—"

"You're disgusting!" Lauren shrieked. "I hate you! You spoil everything! You knew I loved Matt. You *knew* it. But you had to take him, didn't you? You take away everyone I love. But *this*...this is the worst thing you've ever done to me, and I'll never forgive you. Never!"

And then she whirled around and raced out of the kitchen. Pounding upstairs, she nearly fell. When she finally reached the safety of her room, she locked the door behind her, then threw herself facedown across the bed and sobbed her heart out.

Shawn just stood in the middle of the kitchen, frozen. *Dear God,* she thought.

What have we done?

Much later, Lauren heard her mom coming upstairs. Her footsteps stopped outside Lauren's door. Lauren didn't move. When she knocked on the door, Lauren ignored her.

"Lauren, sweetheart, please open the door. Please talk to me."

I never want to talk to her again, Lauren thought. *Maybe the divorce wasn't all Dad's fault. Maybe he had a good reason for turning to Alexandra.* "Go away," she finally said when her mother wouldn't quit knocking. "I have nothing to say to you."

"Lauren, please…"

But Lauren refused to utter another word, even though she could tell her mom had been crying, and finally her mom gave up and went back downstairs. When Lauren was sure she was gone, she picked up her cell phone. She hadn't charged it in two nights, but there was enough battery juice left to make one call.

She punched in the familiar number of her dad's apartment. *Please be home, Daddy.*

A moment later, her dad said, "Hello?"

"Daddy?" Although she tried not to, Lauren started to cry.

"Lauren?"

"D-Daddy," she wept. "Please let me come and live with you and Alexandra. Please?"

"What's wrong, Lauren? What's happened?"

"I don't want to live with Mom anymore. I want to live with you. Please, Daddy, please come and get me!" She knew her father was mystified, but she couldn't talk about what had happened. Couldn't admit that her own mother had stolen the man she loved. It hurt too much.

"But Lauren, honey, you just got home."

"If you don't come to get me, I'll run away, I swear I will."

"Calm down, honey. Of course I'll come. Give me an hour, though. We just sat down to eat."

"Hurry, okay? I'll be waiting for you outside."

Now that she knew she didn't have to stay there, Lauren felt calm. After they hung up, she began to pack the rest of her things, since her stuff from camp was still in her duffel and tote. She wished she could take her computer, but right now, that wasn't possible. Later she'd send her dad back to get it. Her desk, too. 'Cause she was never coming back here. Never.

When fifty minutes had gone by, she started looking out the window and watching for her dad. It seemed to take forever for him to come, but finally his silver Lexus pulled into the driveway.

Shoving her cell phone into her purse, she grabbed her suitcase, duffel bag and tote, and hurried downstairs. Her mom obviously heard her, for she was there waiting for Lauren at the foot of the stairs.

"Lauren? Where are you going?"

"I'm going to Dad's," Lauren said coldly. She hardened her heart against the look on her mother's face. "And I'm not coming back."

Her mom looked as if Lauren had struck her.

"Lauren, sweetheart, this is crazy. Can't we talk about this?"

By now Lauren's dad was at the front door. Lauren opened it. "I'm ready," she said.

Shoving past her mother, she marched outside.

She didn't look back.

Chapter Eleven

"What the hell's going on here, Shawn?" Rick muttered, looking back to make sure Lauren didn't hear him.

"It's just...we had a fight. She's upset with me."

"Well, *hello,* I figured that much out for myself."

"Look, Rick, I—I can't explain right now. And...and this is only temporary."

"It had better be, because Alexandra isn't pleased. Hell, Shawn, we really don't have a place for Lauren, you know that. We're living in a two-bedroom apartment right now, and that second bedroom is going to be the nursery."

Shawn was heartsick.

Watching as Rick drove away—with Lauren in the passenger seat not looking at Shawn—she felt as if she were a total failure as a mother. The last thing she'd ever wanted to do was hurt Lauren, but she had.

And now her baby was leaving.

Shawn wished she knew what to do. Should she have tried harder to keep Lauren there?

On the other hand, maybe it was good that Lauren *had* gone. Maybe they both just needed some time to think, and when Lauren was calmer, they could talk.

We'll work this out, Shawn told herself. *We have to. Anything else is unthinkable.*

Closing the door, Shawn walked slowly back to the kitchen. The grease-stained pizza box sitting on the counter was a cruel reminder of how happy and hopeful she'd felt coming home tonight.

She sank down onto a kitchen chair. Looked around. The house was so quiet. Had that clock hanging on the wall always sounded this loud? Even Trixie wasn't making a sound.

Oh, Lauren, Lauren, I'm so sorry, baby...,

Shawn closed her eyes and took a deep breath.

This will *pass. It will.*

Just then the phone rang, shattering the silence, and Shawn got up to answer it. She hoped it wasn't Matt. She needed some time to think and regroup before she talked to him.

But it was Zoe's number on the caller ID.

Punching Talk, Shawn listlessly said, "Hi, Zoe."

"Well, that's not a very cheery greeting," Zoe said. "What's wrong?"

"It's that obvious?"

"Well, yeah, when you sound as if you just lost your best friend, which happens to be *me*, yeah, it's obvious something's going on."

"Oh, Zoe. I've screwed up so bad. Lauren just left."

"Lauren just left? What's the deal? I thought she just got home today."

"She did, but something awful happened, and she packed her things and now she's gone to stay with Rick and Alexandra."

Zoe listened quietly as Shawn gave her a blow-by-blow of her confrontation with Lauren. When Shawn finished, Zoe said, "Oh, Shawn, I'm so sorry."

"Yeah, me, too."

"What are you going to do?"

"I don't know. I don't have a lot of choices. She won't talk to me." Despair made Shawn's shoulders sag. "She said this is the worst thing I've ever done to her and that she'll never forgive me."

"Shawn, she's a teenage girl. They all act like Sarah Bernhardt."

"I know, I know, but this is different, Zoe. If you could have seen her face. Oh, God, I can't even describe the way she looked. The way she looked *at* me." Tears welled in Shawn's eyes. "She hates me."

"She doesn't hate you. Right now she's very angry with you, and that's a whole different thing."

"I hope you're right."

"Believe me, I am. You know, I've gone through some stuff with Emma in the past, but we've gotten over it."

"Nothing like this, though. I mean, you didn't steal the man she loved."

Zoe chuckled. "No, but she thinks I've stolen something even bigger."

"Her father."

"Yep. Anyway, periodically we have a knockout, drag out, and scream at each other, then in a few days, she gets over it, and things are smooth again. That's what'll happen with you and Lauren, too. You just have to be patient."

Shawn nodded. Patient. Such an easy word to say. Such a hard one to live.

"Have you told Matt yet?" Zoe asked.

"No. But I'll have to call him soon."

Zoe sighed. "Lauren *will* get over this, you know. I mean, teenagers get crushes all the time, and they think it's the end of the world when the romance doesn't survive, but they live through it."

"I know, but somehow this seems different." *What's different is her mother betrayed her.* The thought made it hurt to breathe. She *had* betrayed Lauren. No two ways about it. Even though Lauren had never put her feelings for Matt into words, Shawn had known how her daughter felt.

Oh, God. What was I thinking?

The trouble was, she hadn't *been* thinking. She'd allowed her need to believe she was still attractive and desirable to override her good sense. And when she *had* started thinking about how her relationship with Matt would affect Lauren, by then it was too late, because Shawn had fallen in love with him.

"Shawn, don't beat up on yourself too much. I know this seems insurmountable right now, but things will calm down. Lauren will come around. I guarantee you she won't like living with Rick and Alexandra."

"That's another thing. Rick acted as if he didn't want her. I hope he doesn't let her know he feels this way. Bad enough her mother's let her down. She doesn't need to have her father let her down, too."

"You're a better man than I am, Shawn, because I'd be hoping the creep shows his true colors so Lauren will realize just how great her mother really *is*."

Shawn couldn't help smiling. Zoe was such a good friend. She always took Shawn's side.

They talked a while longer, and when they'd finished their conversation, Shawn knew it was time to call Matt. She couldn't put off telling him about Lauren. It wasn't fair, especially when she knew what she had to do now. Before she lost her courage, she punched in his number.

"Shawn?" he said, answering on the first ring.

"Hi, Matt. Listen, is it all right if I come over?"

"Well, sure, but…uh, isn't Lauren there?"

"No. I'll tell you about it when I get there, okay?"

Shawn changed from her work clothes into shorts and a T-shirt then, deciding it was silly to drive when she could walk to his house in less than five minutes, grabbed her purse and headed out.

Matt was sitting on the porch railing when she arrived, a bottle of beer in his hand. He took one look at her face and knew something was very wrong.

"What happened?" he said.

"Let's go inside, okay?"

"Sure."

Inside he said, "Would you like a beer?"

Shawn shook her head.

"Let's at least go sit down in the living room."

"All right." She sat on the sofa and he sat beside her.

"Tell me," he said.

As she talked, his heart sank.

"Ah, Shawn, I'm sorry," he said when she'd finished telling him about the scene with Lauren and its aftermath. Seeing the tears in her eyes, he tried to put his arms around her.

"Please, Matt, don't." She moved away. "Don't make this harder for me."

He froze. "Make what harder?"

Her unhappy gaze met his. "I—I just think it's best if we don't see each other for a while."

A tear trembled on the edge of her lashes, and it was all he could do to keep from wiping it away. "Shawn," he said softly. "Please don't shut me out. I love you. We love each other. We can't let this come between us. Why don't we do what I wanted to do before? Talk to Lauren together? She's a sensible kid. Sure, she's hurt right now, but she'll come around."

She shook her head. "No. That's not a good idea. She already feels betrayed. If she had to face you, she'd be mortified. I can't do that to her."

"Okay, maybe that's not such a good idea. But I really think all she needs is time."

"I hope so."

"Tell me again why we have to stop seeing each other. How will that help anything?"

"I just…I just can't, Matt. Not now. Not until Lauren is okay with it."

Matt couldn't help it. He was hurt. "I can't believe you're doing this, Shawn. I know you love Lauren, but I can't believe you're ready to throw away what we have together because she has a stupid crush on me."

"Do you think this is easy for me?" she cried. "It's not what I want."

"Then don't do it."

"You don't understand. She's my *child!* She has to come first."

Suddenly he felt cold all over. What was she saying?

That Lauren would always come first? That what he felt didn't matter?

"Matt, I'm sorry. I know what you're thinking. But you don't have children, so you don't understand."

He stared at her.

"Matt, don't look at me that way."

Affecting a nonchalance he didn't feel, he shrugged. "It's probably a good thing this happened. At least now I know exactly where I stand."

School started the Wednesday after Labor Day. By then Lauren had been staying at her father's apartment for almost three weeks.

They'd been tough weeks for Shawn. Lauren still refused to talk to her. No matter how many times Shawn called, Lauren wouldn't come to the phone, and if Shawn called Lauren's cell, she simply let the call go to voice mail, and she didn't return it.

Rick had tried talking to her, too, with no more success. He still didn't know the story and, to his credit, he hadn't pressed Shawn for details. Apparently he still remembered his own culpability when it came to Lauren's unhappiness. At any rate, Shawn was grateful for his lack of censure as well as his willingness to have Lauren stay with him until they could get past this problem, for he had had a change of heart, telling Shawn he was sorry he'd acted as if he didn't want Lauren.

"I do want her," he said. "It's just that right now is a

touchy time with Alexandra. You know, with the pregnancy and everything."

What a shame, Shawn thought nastily before her better nature banished the mean thought. Anyway, she didn't want Lauren to suffer as a result of Alexandra's irritability.

This situation was just temporary, Shawn kept assuring herself. Lauren wouldn't be angry forever. She was young. She'd forget about all of this in time, just as she'd get over her crush on Matt.

Matt.

Shawn missed him more than she'd ever have thought possible. She'd wanted to call him so many times, but she'd resisted the temptation, because it wouldn't be fair to him. She knew he was hurt. That he thought she cared for Lauren more than she cared for him.

That wasn't true.

Shawn knew, especially after these three lonely weeks, that she loved Matt every bit as much as she loved Lauren.

But Lauren was her *child!*

Flesh of her flesh, blood of her blood.

She was responsible for Lauren.

The love she felt for Matt was an adult love, whereas the love she felt for Lauren was all mixed up in her fierce need to take care of her daughter, to protect her.

So she didn't call Matt. And the loneliness ate at her.

Some nights she just couldn't face going home to her empty house, the house she'd decorated with such love just a few short months ago.

She spent a lot of time with Zoe and the other members of her Wednesday-night group. And sometimes she simply went to Callie's for dinner by herself when the thought of being alone in the house was too much to bear.

The third time she showed up at Callie's alone, Callie joined her in her booth. "You don't mind, do you?" she asked.

Her warmth and sympathetic gaze were nearly Shawn's undoing. "I'm not the best company right now."

Callie stirred sweetener into her coffee. "Want to tell me about it?"

"You must get sick of hearing people's problems."

Callie grinned. "I'm like a priest that way. It's part of my job to listen."

Shawn laughed. Callie always had that effect on her. "Well, if you're sure you want to listen…"

Callie sighed when Shawn had finished reciting her tale of woe. "Oh, Shawn, that's tough."

Shawn nodded, listlessly stirring the rice around on her plate. "I just…feel so impotent, you know? And I miss Matt dreadfully, but I…" Her voice trailed off. "Do you think I'm doing the right thing?"

Callie shrugged. "I don't know, Shawn. What I do know is if it were Kristie, I'd probably have made the same decision."

"Would you?" It made Shawn feel better just to know another mother felt the same way she did.

"Yes, absolutely." Callie's hazel eyes met Shawn's. "The thing is, Shawn, if Matt really loves you, he'll be patient. If he isn't patient, then the question you should ask yourself is, is he the right man for you? After all, being a mother is an important part of who you are, and he has to understand that."

Shawn nodded again. She knew Callie was right, but she was scared. She didn't know what she'd do if she lost Matt. He'd come to mean so much to her.

Maybe I've already lost him.

This was the thought that had haunted her the past weeks. Because if he *did* really love her, wouldn't he have tried to call her or see her? Sure, she'd said she thought it was best for them not to see each other until this thing with Lauren was resolved, but still…wouldn't he have at least *tried?*

The weeks since Shawn had told him her decision were tough on Matt, too. He was miserable and couldn't believe how much he missed her. He'd gone from being a contented bachelor to being lovesick and lonely.

He tried to keep busy so he wouldn't have time to think. The beginning of the school year was always filled to the brim, so that was good, and in his off hours, he worked on the house, he ran, he went to the gym, and he spent time with Cathy and her family.

Despite all that, there were still too many hours when his mind seemed to have one direction and one direction only.

Shawn.

What would he do if their break was permanent?

Somehow Matt didn't think he'd get over her easily…if at all. In a very short time, she'd gotten under his skin and seemed permanently wedged there.

He wished he could at least talk to Shawn, if only to find out how Lauren was doing. Since she wasn't in any of his classes this semester, he hadn't seen much of her—just an occasional sighting in the hall. He knew she was avoiding him, and he felt bad because he hated that he and Shawn had hurt her.

But hell, what was he supposed to have done to avoid it? He'd fallen for Shawn before he'd had any idea of the depth of Lauren's feelings for him.

If only he could call Shawn. But she had made herself clear. She'd said she didn't feel there should be any contact between them until she'd gotten things under control with Lauren. At first he'd been so angry and hurt, he wouldn't have called her, anyway.

Now, though, he was calmer and had more perspective. And he realized Shawn had really done the only thing she could do, under the circumstances.

So even though he wanted to talk to her, he had to respect her decision about no contact.

But he didn't have to like it.

* * *

Lauren had never been so miserable. Some days she thought her heart had a permanent crack in it and would never be whole again.

Why did it hurt so much to love someone?

Everything was spoiled now. She didn't even like going to school, and school had always been a good place to be. It had been a place to escape when there was a problem at home. And home had been her refuge when things weren't going well at school.

Now neither place was a place she wanted to be. At school she had to pretend nothing was wrong or else be subjected to all kinds of questions from Heather and her other friends. And there was the added fear of accidentally seeing Matt. Not that she talked to him when she did. She pretended she *didn't* see him and got away as soon as she could.

But it hurt. It hurt so bad to see him. Because she couldn't just turn her feelings on and off like a spigot.

Every time she saw him, the hurt was a raw, aching wound again, and she remembered that it was her mother who had caused this misery.

Her mother!

The betrayal still stunned her. How could her mother have done such an awful thing to her? *She must not love me at all.*

Being at her dad's wasn't much better than school, either. Alexandra didn't want her there, Lauren had known that from the moment she'd arrived. And Lauren didn't think her dad really wanted her there, either.

The biggest problem was Alexandra wasn't feeling great. Her feet were swelling and she was sick to her stomach a lot and she was always tired.

And she and Lauren's dad seemed to argue a lot. Lauren had heard them arguing again last night. They were trying to be quiet, but the walls were thin, and Lauren couldn't help hearing them.

Alexandra wanted to quit working and Lauren's dad said they couldn't afford it right now.

"We could afford it if you weren't giving Shawn so much money every month," Alexandra had said.

"We agreed on the money, Alexandra."

Lauren could tell from her dad's tone that he was mad.

"That was before I knew Lauren was going to be *living* with us. And that's another thing. Where are we going to put the *baby* if Lauren stays? She's in the room I planned to use as a nursery."

"Lauren won't be here forever."

"She'd better not be. I didn't sign on for a teenager, Rick."

"Keep your voice down. I don't want her to hear us."

"Well, maybe I do. I'm sick of her moping around here, and I'm sick of you traveling so much, and I'm sick of being pregnant!"

Lauren's stomach hurt. If she had somewhere to go, she'd run away.

But she didn't have anywhere to go.

Because no one wanted her.

When an entire month had gone by and Lauren was still living at Rick's...and still refusing to talk to Shawn, Shawn decided something had to be done. Otherwise, this status quo would go on forever. And that was unacceptable.

But if Lauren wouldn't see her and refused to take her calls, what could she do?

Shawn agonized over the problem for days. Finally she decided her best option was sending Lauren an e-mail. She was sure Lauren would read it, even if she didn't answer it. And that was the best Shawn could hope for right now—to get Lauren's attention.

She started the e-mail at least a dozen times, then discarded what she'd written. Finally she just said what was in her heart:

Dearest Lauren, she wrote.

I know you probably don't believe it, but I love you so much. You're more important to me than anyone or anything in the world, and I'm sorrier than I can ever say that I've hurt you. I never intended to, and I promise I will never hurt you like this again. I just wanted you to know how much I miss you. And I wanted you to know that I'm not seeing Matt anymore and I'm not planning to start seeing him again.

I hope you can forgive me, because I want you to come home. Please come home, Lauren. Please.

Love, Mom

Shawn closed her eyes, whispered a prayer, then pushed Send.

Lauren went to the library after her last class. It had gotten so anyplace was better than going home. Since one of the computers was free, she claimed it, logged on to Web mail and typed in her password to access her e-mail account. Lately Doug Fields had been writing to her and, in spite of not wanting him to think she was interested in him, she found herself looking forward to his posts. Since he didn't know anything about what had happened with her and her mom and Matt, she found she could just relax and talk to him, which was a huge relief, since she couldn't talk to anyone else right now.

She smiled when she saw his name in her in-box. Then the smile turned into a frown. There was also an e-mail from her mother. Scrolling down, she highlighted her mother's post and almost hit the delete button. Just in time, she stopped herself. Curiosity got the better of her. It wouldn't hurt anything just to read what her mother had to say. It wasn't as if her mother ever had to *know,* and Lauren certainly didn't have to answer it or even acknowledge that she'd gotten it.

She opened the e-mail.

Her heart began to pound as she read.

I promise I will never hurt you like this again. I just wanted you to know how much I miss you. And I wanted you to know that I'm not seeing Matt anymore.

Lauren's eyes filled with tears. She wanted to believe her mom. Wanted to desperately.

I want you to come home. Please come home, Lauren. Please.

"Home," Lauren whispered around the ache in her heart.

That night she couldn't sleep. She kept thinking about what her mom had written. The next day, after school, Lauren didn't get on the school bus. Instead she bummed a ride with Heather and her mother, who dropped her at her mom's office.

"Lauren!" her mom said when Lauren walked in. She smiled hesitantly.

Lauren swallowed. "Hi."

"Come in. Sit down." Her mom pointed to the chairs along the wall. "Pull one up to the desk."

Lauren nodded. When she was seated next to her mom's desk, she said, "I got your e-mail."

Her mom's smile was so hopeful. "Did you?"

"Yeah. I…" She took a deep breath. "Did you mean what you said?"

"I meant every word, honey."

"You really won't see Matt again?"

Her mom shook her head. "No. I won't."

"Okay then. I—I want to come home."

Her mother reached across the desk and clasped Lauren's hand. "Oh, Lauren, I'm so glad. I've missed you so much."

Swallowing against the lump in her throat, Lauren said, "I've missed you, too."

Chapter Twelve

Shawn put off calling Matt. She knew she had to, knew it wasn't fair to keep him in the dark about what she had decided to do. Yet somehow, not telling him made it less real. As long as she didn't give Matt an official good-bye, then there was always hope that something might change.

But down deep Shawn knew nothing was going to change. How could it? She was just putting off the inevitable.

So three days after Lauren returned home, when she had gone to her karate class and wouldn't be back for at least an hour and a half, Shawn grabbed her jacket, put Trixie on a lead and left the house.

Approaching Matt's house, she said a quick prayer. *Please let me get through this without crying. Please let me keep it together until I get home.*

Her heart was beating double time as she tied Trixie to the porch railing and then walked up to Matt's front door. With trembling fingers, she rang the bell. *Maybe he's not home.* It was part fear, part hope.

She had just about decided she'd been given a reprieve, that he *wasn't* home, when the door opened.

"Shawn!" His warm brown eyes—oh, she loved his eyes!—lit up.

Her heart knocked painfully. It hurt to see the joy on his face. *Oh, Matt, I'm so sorry.* Somehow she managed to speak calmly. "Hi, Matt. May I come in?"

"Of course. What about Trixie? Want to bring her in?"

"No, she's fine out here. I—I can't stay long."

Her tone must have alerted him to the fact this wasn't going to be the kind of visit he wanted, for his smile slipped and his eyes became wary. "So what brings you here?"

Shawn took a deep breath for courage. "Lauren's home again."

"Well, that's good, isn't it?"

"Yes, but…she only came home because I made her a promise."

His gaze locked with hers. A long, silent moment went by. "I see," he finally said.

"Matt, this isn't what I want…."

"Why don't you just tell me what you promised," he said flatly.

"I—" Why was it so hard to get the words out?

He looked at her for what seemed an eternity. "I guess you've answered my question."

"I'd hoped things could be different, but…" Shawn swallowed. "Lauren will never accept you. And I can't—"

"You don't have to say it. I get the picture," he said, cutting her off. After a moment, he sighed deeply. "I'm sorry, too, Shawn. Sorrier than you'll ever know."

Tears filled Shawn's eyes. "Matt…" She reached out, but he ignored her hand. It fell to her side. Her heart felt splintered. Nothing had ever hurt this much.

Turning, she murmured, "Goodbye, Matt. I-I'll never forget you."

She'd already opened the door and was halfway outside when he covered the space between them in two long strides, grabbed her arm, and pulled her back inside and into his arms.

His kiss was fierce, and she clung to him and returned it with everything that was in her heart, everything she was feeling but couldn't say.

When he realized she was crying, he cradled her head against his chest and held her. "I'll always love you, Shawn," he said in a ragged voice.

The tears came harder now and, when she finally

pulled away, she saw there were tears in his eyes, too. Knowing she had to get away or she'd do something she shouldn't, Shawn blurted out, "I'll never forget you," then bolted out the door.

Her hands were shaking so hard, she struggled to untie Trixie's lead, but finally she got it undone. She practically ran down the street. Only when she'd rounded the corner and knew she was out of sight of Matt's house did she slow down. She was crying so hard she could hardly see, but she didn't wipe the tears away. They were her badge of honor. Along with her memories, they were all she had left of Matt.

"Matt, what's wrong?"

The concerned question came from Cathy, who'd been watching him ever since he'd arrived for dinner two hours earlier. Matt knew she'd been wanting to ask it ever since, but she'd considerately waited until the kids had gone off to do whatever it was kids did on Sunday afternoons and Lowell had retreated to the basement to finish the cradle he was making for his kid sister, who was expecting her first baby.

Matt sighed. "It's Shawn. We broke up."

"Oh, Matt, I'm sorry." Cathy began to dry the dishes she'd just washed.

"Thanks."

"Maybe…" Her voice trailed off.

Matt looked up. "Maybe what?"

She shrugged. "Look, maybe it's for the best. I mean, she'd older than you, and you want kids…."

Glumly, Matt acknowledged the truth of what Cathy had said. But that truth was nothing compared to the truth of what he felt for Shawn, the truth of what they meant to each other, and the truth of what they could have built together.

"If I was out of line, Matt, I'm sorry," Cathy said when he didn't answer her comment.

He shook his head. "No, it's okay, I know you're only thinking of what's best for me, but the thing is, I don't think I'm going to get over this easily." The truth was he wasn't sure he was going to get over Shawn at all. And yet, what other choice did he have?

"Some things just take more time than others, but we get over everything eventually."

He nodded, but he wasn't sure. He'd thought he'd been hurt when Sarah had broken their engagement, but that was nothing compared to this—a bruise as opposed to an amputation.

"I'm not sure I'm going to stay here," he said.

"Oh, Matt. You wouldn't leave Maple Hills, would you? I love having you here! And so do the kids."

"I know. I love being close to you guys, too, but Cath, I'm not sure I can stand being in the same town with Shawn. This isn't like Cleveland. Maple Hills is small. I'm bound to run into her over and over again. I—I don't think I can do it."

Cathy's face fell. Putting down her dish towel, she pulled a chair out and sat across from him. "Oh, Matt, I'm sorry. I was being selfish, thinking about how I feel instead of how you feel. But…if you go, *where* will you go?"

"I've been thinking about that. Maybe I'll just take a year off. Volunteer for the Peace Corps. They still need teachers badly. And I've always wanted to do something like that. Maybe this is the time."

Cathy didn't say anything for a while. Finally she reached across the table and squeezed his hand. "All I have to say is, your Shawn is crazy. Guys like you don't come along twice in a lifetime."

Matt leaned over and kissed her cheek. "I love you, too, kid."

Lauren was glad to be home, but it wasn't the same as it had been. Her mom was trying hard, but it was obvious to Lauren that her mother was unhappy.

At times Lauren felt guilty, but then she'd get mad at herself. Why should *she* feel guilty? She hadn't done anything wrong. Her mom was the one who should feel guilty.

Well, at least *Alexandra* was happy. She hadn't even tried to hide her feelings when Lauren had told her dad that she was going to move back home.

"That's a good decision, Lauren," she'd said. "It's too crowded here for you to have any privacy, and once the baby comes, it'll be even worse."

Yeah, Lauren had thought, *you're not worried about my privacy, you're worried about your own.* Of course, she hadn't said that. She'd just nodded and let Alexandra think she agreed with her.

Funny how much she'd liked Alexandra when all she'd been was her dad's assistant—before Lauren had found out about their affair. Now she saw Alexandra in an entirely different light, and she wasn't crazy about what she saw. In fact, she still couldn't figure out why her father had preferred Alexandra to her mom.

Thing is, Alexandra whined. There was no other word for it. Lauren didn't care for people who whined. It was one of the reasons she'd been trying to distance herself from Heather and spend more time with other friends. And Lauren didn't think her dad was going to put up with Alexandra's whining if it continued after the baby was born, either. But that wasn't Lauren's problem.

It was her dad's.

Lauren was going home.

On Monday, after his last class, Matt headed for the principal's office.

"Come in," she called out after he'd knocked.

Matt liked Michele Post and hoped she wouldn't hold what he was going to tell her against him.

She waved him to a seat, saying, "Hello, Matt. What's on your mind?"

He could tell how disappointed she was as he explained that something unforeseen had happened, and he needed to leave at the end of the semester.

"Oh, Matt, we'll hate to lose you."

"Thank you. I hate to go, but it can't be helped."

"You're sure you won't change your mind?"

"I'm sure."

"Well, then, I wish you luck. And I want you to know that if you ever want to come back, we'd love to have you."

"That means a lot to me."

They shook hands and Matt left.

Although his heart was still heavy, it seemed to have lightened just a bit. He knew he was doing the right thing. For him…and for Shawn.

"Hey, Lauren, did you hear?"

"Hear what?" Lauren said to Heather, who had just caught up with her on the way to English Lit.

"About Mr. McFarland."

Even the sound of his name could make Lauren's heart skip. "What about Mr. McFarland?" she said carefully.

"He's leaving." Heather made a face. "I knew it was too good to be true that we could have a hot young guy for a teacher. Now we'll probably get some horse-faced old witch in his place."

Lauren bit her lip. Why was he going away? Did it

have anything to do with her mom and her? She wondered if her mother knew.

For the rest of the afternoon, his leaving was all Lauren could think about.

Lauren had been voted to the student council this year, and there was a meeting after school. It lasted till after four-thirty, then some of the kids invited her to go to Burger Barn for a Coke, and Lauren decided to go. By the time she got home, her mom was already there.

Their relationship was still strained, but both of them were trying hard to pretend it wasn't.

"I thought I'd just make some hamburgers tonight," her mom said. "And a salad to go with them. Is that okay with you?"

"Sure."

"Are you real hungry now?"

Lauren shook her head. "I had a Coke and some chips at Burger Barn."

"Then I'll just go change clothes and maybe do thirty minutes on the treadmill before I start supper."

"Um, Mom, before you go, I was wondering…did you know Ma—Mr. McFarland is leaving at the end of the semester?"

For a moment, her mom looked as if someone had hit her. "N-no, I didn't. Who…who told you this?"

"It's all over school. Apparently he's joining the Peace Corps. He told one of the kids he's hoping to work in Peru."

"Well," her mom said—she'd recovered her equilibrium now and her expression was calm. "He'll be good at that. I wish him luck."

"Yeah," Lauren said, but inside she felt something entirely different. And she knew her mom did, too.

Shawn held herself together until she got to her bedroom. But once the door was shut, she began to shake.

Leaving.

Matt was leaving.

Now the last sliver of hope she'd harbored that one day Lauren might have a change of heart and there would still be a chance for Shawn and Matt disappeared.

It's over, she thought in despair.

I'll never see him again.

That night Lauren heard her mother crying. It was a soft sound, and she knew her mom had no idea Lauren could hear, but she did. It made Lauren feel bad, and then she got mad at herself. Why should *she* feel bad? She hadn't done anything. It was her mom who had caused the problems, and now she was suffering the consequences. Wasn't that what she was always preaching to Lauren? That we're responsible for our actions?

Lauren tossed and turned. She couldn't seem to get comfortable and she had a hard time falling asleep. She finally did, but not before making a decision.

The next morning, she went to school early, telling her mom she had promised Annie Campbell she'd meet her in the library to study for their French test. But when she got to the school, she headed straight for Matt's room. He was always there at least half an hour before his first class started, and she hoped today was no exception. But even if he wasn't there this morning, she was determined to talk to him sometime today, even if she had to wait until this afternoon when school was over.

The light was on in his room and, through the frosted window in the door, she could see him sitting at his desk. Her heart thumped painfully. Suddenly too nervous to follow through with her plan, she almost turned around and walked away. Then, telling herself not to be a wimp, she took a deep breath and knocked.

"Yes?" he called.

She opened the door a crack. "M-Mr. McFarland?"

"Lauren!" He stood. "Come in."

She could see he was happy to see her, and it made her feel better. At least he didn't hate her! She walked into the room and closed the door. "I—I wanted to talk to you about something."

"Well, come and sit down."

She walked over to the first row of chairs and sat. He came to the front of his desk and sat on the edge. "I'm glad to see you," he said.

"I—I heard you're leaving," she said around the pain in her heart. "Is it true?"

His eyes met hers, and in them she saw sympathy and understanding. "Yes, it's true."

She wanted to cry. "I thought you liked it here."

"I do. I like it very much."

"Then why are you going?"

He sighed. When he finally spoke, his voice was gentle. "I love your mother, Lauren. I wanted to marry her, to be part of your family. But she said you're the most important person in her life, and if we were to marry it would hurt you. So she decided it would be best if we broke it off and didn't see each other anymore. That's why I think it's best if I go away now. It'll be easier on everyone. Maybe once I'm gone you and your mother can have the kind of relationship you once had. I hope so."

Lauren didn't know what to say. "I'm…I'm sorry," she finally got out.

He smiled gently. "I'm sorry, too."

"W-when are you going?"

"After the holidays, before the new semester begins."

"Do you think you'll ever come back?"

He shook his head.

"I—I wish you weren't leaving."

"Thank you. That means a lot to me."

Lauren fought against the tears that threatened. "I thought you'd hate me."

"I could never hate you, Lauren. You're a wonderful girl. I would have been proud to be your stepfather."

Lauren bit her lip. She was terribly afraid she was going to cry. She stood. She had to get out of there before she made a fool of herself.

He stood, too.

"I know that someday you'll meet someone perfect for you," he said softly. She knew he meant *someone your age*. "Take care of your mother, okay? She's been hurt a lot. She doesn't deserve to be hurt anymore."

Lauren barely got out the door before the tears she'd managed to suppress in his classroom erupted. She made a beeline for the nearest girls' restroom where she locked herself in a stall and cried her heart out.

When she was finally calm again, she left the stall and went to the sink where she splashed cold water on her face. Then she blew her nose, put on fresh lip gloss, brushed her hair and inspected herself in the mirror.

If no one looked too closely, she'd be okay.

On the outside, that is.

Inside was another story.

Poor kid, Matt thought as he watched her leave. He had a feeling she was just beginning to realize the misery she'd caused. And yet, was any of what had happened really all Lauren's fault? Didn't he and Shawn have to bear at least half the responsibility? They should have been up-front about their relationship from the very beginning. Maybe if they had been, Lauren would have reacted differently.

He'd wanted to ask her about Shawn, but he hadn't wanted to add to her discomfort.

He sighed, put his head in his hands.

Why did life have to be so damned hard?

Shawn knew she had to shape up. And the first step would be to stop at the supermarket on her way home from work and buy enough food so that she could actually put some decent meals on the table in the next few days. She'd served enough hamburgers and take-out Chinese to Lauren since she'd come back.

She scribbled a list right before five, but by the time she reached the supermarket parking lot, she'd thought of at least a dozen more things she needed.

She was in the middle of the produce department, trying to pick out a good-looking head of romaine lettuce when suddenly, out of the corner of her eye, she saw a man who looked exactly like Matt.

Oh, God. It *was* Matt.

He was standing by a bin of Gala apples. He hadn't seen her.

She whirled around so that her back was to him. Her heart was racing in panic.

What should I do? I can't face him. Not here. Not now.

She'd leave.

So what if she fed Lauren takeout again tonight?

Afraid to turn around, she groped blindly behind

herself until she felt the straps of her purse, which she'd placed in the child seat part of her basket. She tugged, but the straps were caught and she couldn't remove the purse without looking. Cautiously, she glanced around. And just as she did, Matt turned.

Their eyes met.

"Shawn."

She couldn't actually hear him say her name, but she saw his lips form the word. She somehow managed to smile and wave.

He immediately walked over.

"Hello, Matt." She sounded so normal. No one would ever guess she was falling apart inside.

"Hello, Shawn."

He smiled, but his eyes betrayed him and she knew he was as shaken by this encounter as she was.

"How have you been?" she asked.

"I'm okay. You?"

"I'm fine." She was filled with helpless longing for all that would never be.

"I've missed you," he said softly.

Her heart seized up. "Oh, Matt, I've missed you, too."

For a long moment, they said nothing else. A flood of emotion swamped her. She wanted to say something about his leaving, but she couldn't get the words out.

Finally he spoke. "Lauren came to see me today."

"She did?"

He nodded. "Yes. She wanted to know if I was really leaving Maple Hills." He smiled crookedly. "I'd forgotten how fast news travels in a small town."

Shawn swallowed. "So is it true?"

"Yes, the rumors are true. I gave the principal my resignation last week."

Hearing him confirm what Lauren had told her was as painful as hearing it the first time.

"That wasn't all Lauren wanted," he said. "She also wanted to know why I was going."

Shawn stared at him. Her heart was pounding as if she'd run a mile. "What did you tell her?"

"I told her I was going because I love you and we can't be together and I think it'll be easier for both of us for me to be gone."

Oh, God. She was going to cry again. What was wrong with her that lately she seemed to cry at the drop of a hat?

He reached for her hand and lifted it to his mouth. The touch of his lips against her palm sent shivers down her spine. "Take care of yourself, Shawn."

Then without another word, he released her hand, turned and walked away.

Chapter Thirteen

For the rest of the day, Lauren could think of nothing else but her conversation with Matt.

I love your mother. I wanted to marry her. I would have been proud to be your stepfather.

Those words in particular wouldn't let her go. She kept thinking about the look on Matt's face when he'd said them. She could see that he'd been sincere. That he was hurt by what had happened and that he missed her mom.

Then she thought about her dad and Alexandra and how they had betrayed and hurt her mother. She thought about the baby they were having and remembered how much her mother had wanted another child and how her eyes would get all wistful and sad every time she'd see a baby. She thought about how her mother had never said anything bad about her father, even when she could have.

The more Lauren thought about everything, the worse she felt. She was glad she had a karate lesson after school. At least then, she'd have something else to think about.

But throughout the various stances, kicks and punches practiced that afternoon, she couldn't maintain the discipline and single-mindedness she needed to perform at her best. The instructor noticed. Several times he corrected her or made her repeat a move.

Afterward, as she and Annie were waiting for Annie's mother—who was running late—to pick them up, Annie said, "Is something wrong, Lauren?"

Lauren wanted so badly to tell Annie everything. Yet she held back. What would Annie think of her?

"You can tell me," Annie said, "I won't tell anyone else."

Lauren sighed. "It's not that. I know you wouldn't. It's just that I'm embarrassed to tell you."

Annie didn't push. She wasn't like that. She just stood quietly.

Lauren toed the grass at the end of the parking lot. Both girls were still dressed in their white uniforms with their green belts knotted tightly. "Remember when you told me about my mom and Mr. McFarland and how you saw them kissing?"

"Yeah."

"Well…" Lauren sighed again, then went on to tell Annie everything.

When she'd finished, Annie sighed, too. "Oh, Lauren, I can't believe this. It's…it's like a *movie!*"

"Yeah," Lauren said glumly. "A horror story."

"No, it's sad, I mean."

Neither girl said anything for a minute.

"Do you think I'm a jerk?" Lauren finally said.

"No. Why would I think that?"

Lauren shrugged. "'Cause maybe I am."

"Hey, you fell in love, just like your mom did."

Lauren looked at Annie to see if she was making fun of her. But her friend's expression was sincere. "He was always way too old for me."

"I know. But we can't help who we love. So what are you gonna do?"

"I don't know. That's what I'm trying to figure out."

"Would it be so bad if your mom and Mr. McFarland *did* get back together?" Annie said.

The question haunted Lauren all the way home. She got there a little after five. Her mom wasn't home from work yet, so Lauren headed upstairs to her bedroom. *Would* it be so bad if Matt and her mom got back together?

Still pondering the answer, she sat down and booted up her computer, then checked her e-mail. She was pleased when she saw a post from Doug. Clicking it open, she read:

Hey, Lauren, I was glad to get your e-mail and to find out you're not going with that older guy anymore. So, anyway, I was thinking. How'd you like to come to Fairfield for homecoming? You could stay over on Friday—share my sister's room—you'll like Liz—she's lots of fun—and then we could do some stuff on Saturday and I'll bring you home on Saturday night. Well, my Dad will be doing the driving, and my mom will probably ride along, but it'll be fun. What do you say?

Lauren stared at the e-mail. Then, for the first time in days, in weeks, she grinned…and really meant it.

Shawn was a wreck. She did manage to pull herself together long enough to call Lauren and tell her she'd be late, then get the groceries she needed, but she wasn't operating at full capacity. She was still too shell-shocked and sad from the encounter with Matt.

By the time she'd paid for her groceries and driven home it was well after six. She dreaded facing Lauren. It had been hard enough just talking to her on the phone.

When she walked into the kitchen, she was shocked to find Lauren there making chili and humming. Tears filled Shawn's eyes. It was so good to see her daughter acting normal. Acting happy. What was going on? "Hi, honey," she said tentatively.

Lauren grinned. "Hi, Mom."

"What's the occasion?"

"The chili, you mean?"

The chili. The humming. The smile. "Yes," Shawn said. She was afraid to say anything else in case the spell was broken.

"Oh, Mom," Lauren said, "so much has happened to me today! I have so much to tell you."

Shawn listened, stunned and afraid to trust the hope and excitement that built as Lauren talked.

But when Lauren finished and said, "Mom, I was wrong. If you and M-Matt want to be together, I'm... I'm okay with it."

Shawn's eyes filled with tears. She opened her arms and Lauren came into them. They hugged and cried and hugged some more.

Things weren't perfect, Shawn knew that, and things wouldn't necessarily be easy, either, but at least they'd made a beginning. At least they were going to try.

Later that night, Matt was listening to music and thinking about Shawn. He couldn't forget the look in her eyes when they'd met at the supermarket. He hoped she was doing better than he was. He felt as if someone had kicked him in the stomach every time he remembered saying goodbye to her.

Gotta stop thinking. It's not productive.

Productive.

What a ridiculous word.

Who cared if thinking about Shawn wasn't productive? Who wanted to be productive, anyway?

He had just gotten up to put on another CD when there was a knock at his door.

He frowned. Crap. He wasn't in the mood to see anyone. Who could it be, anyway? He wasn't expecting company. Maybe he'd just ignore the knock. Pretend he wasn't home. Immediately he realized how stupid that was. The lights were on. Mozart was playing. Whoever was on the other side of the door, they already knew he was there.

Sighing, he walked to the foyer and opened the door. For a moment, he just stood there, frozen.

"Shawn!" he finally said.

Her smile said she was scared.

"What is it? What's happened?"

"Oh, Matt. I can hardly believe it."

Taking her arm, he brought her inside. "Believe what?" His heart pounded. Something terrible must have happened.

"Lauren. It's Lauren." Shawn's eyes filled with tears.

Jesus, he thought.

"She told me tonight that if…if we still wanted to be together, she was okay with it."

At first he wasn't sure he'd heard her correctly.

"Is it too late for us?" she asked.

Belatedly, he realized her tears were ones of joy, not sorrow.

In answer, he scooped her into his arms. He kissed her like a man dying of thirst who has finally been given a drink. Salty tears mixed with the sweetness of her mouth. They kissed for a long time.

When they finally came up for air, he smoothed her hair back from her face and looked down into her eyes.

"I love you, Shawn."

"And I love you."

"I have just one question."

Her smile was radiant. "Okay."

Grinning, he said, "I think elopements are best. What do you say to next week?"

Shawn awakened slowly on the morning of her wedding day. Although the blinds in her bedroom were closed, she knew it was going to be a gorgeous day. How could it be anything else? Today she would marry the love of her life.

She was glad she'd talked Matt out of eloping. At first it had sounded good, just running off and getting married and telling everyone after the fact.

Then she'd thought about Lauren.

And her buddies in the Wednesday Night Gang.

And Matt's sister and her family. Not to mention the rest of his family in Cleveland.

Wouldn't she and Matt regret not having all the people who loved them there to witness them pledging their love and lives to one another?

So they'd compromised. Matt agreed to a wedding and reception, and Shawn agreed they would keep everything simple and small and it would take place as soon as possible.

So here she was, on the second Saturday in November, less than a month after reconciling with Matt, on the threshold of a new life.

She smiled thinking how she used to believe—when she'd been married to Rick and living in her dream house—that she had the perfect life. In fact, her friends had teased her all the time, saying things like, "How would Shawn know? She doesn't have any problems. Her life is perfect."

Well, her life hadn't been perfect. The perfection had been a facade, albeit one she'd believed in.

But now…now she really was headed toward the closest thing to perfection she could imagine. Because Matt was everything and more than she'd ever hoped for in a man. And each day she discovered new facets to his personality. Sure, he had his faults. Everyone did. But even his faults were endearing.

"Just wait a while," Zoe had said when Shawn had expressed that sentiment the previous Wednesday night. "Sure, he seems wonderful now, but what about ten years from now? Trust me, honey child, you won't think he's so perfect then."

"Don't listen to her, Shawn," Susan had said, laughing. "Zoe's completely jaded, and you know it."

"Show me a perfect man, and I'll show you a woman," Zoe had quipped.

"Oh, Zoe!" Carol had said.

"Mom!" Emma had said.

They'd all laughed.

"What about Orlando Bloom?" Ann had teased. They all knew about Zoe's obsession with the gorgeous actor.

"To every rule there is an exception," Zoe had said.

Shawn grinned and stretched. It was time to get up and get ready for her big day.

Twenty minutes later, teeth brushed, face washed, hair combed, she was in the kitchen with a fragrant mug of coffee in her hands. The sun was up now, and the entire eastern horizon shone pink and gold. Standing by her kitchen window, she looked out at the frost-covered lawn, which sparkled with a thousand pinpoints of light. While she watched, a cardinal landed on the lip of the bird bath Matt had bought her, its scarlet plumage an exclamation point of color against the drab stone.

Oh, what a beautiful morning... The song from *Oklahoma!* drifted through her mind.

"Mom?"

Shawn turned to see a sleepy-eyed Lauren standing in the doorway. "Good morning, sweetie."

Lauren rubbed her eyes. "What time is Zoe coming?"

"Zoe and Emma will both be here by nine."

It was now seven. The wedding was scheduled for noon in the chapel at Shawn's church, followed by a buffet lunch at Matt's sister's house. All of Matt's family were now in Maple Hills. His parents were staying at Cathy's. His sister Paula and her husband, Mitch, were staying in Matt's guest room. His brother, John, and his family had a room at a local motel, as did his sister Amy and her fiancé, Jack.

Shawn was thrilled to be marrying into such a large, close-knit family. As an only child, she'd always envied friends with siblings. There were times she'd have given anything to have had a sister or brother to confide in…or even to argue with.

But she'd been destined to be an only chick, just as Lauren had been for so long. But that would soon change, she thought. Alexandra's baby would be born right before Christmas. It no longer bothered Shawn that she'd been pregnant even before Rick and Shawn were divorced. Now that Shawn had Matt, she didn't begrudge Alexandra a thing.

"Are you excited, Mom?" Lauren said. She'd walked over to the stove and put the kettle on. Lately Lauren had taken to drinking hot tea in the morning.

Shawn smiled. "Yes. Nervous, too."

"Nervous? Why?"

"Why are you nervous before a big test?"

Lauren grinned. "But this is different. You love Matt."

"Doesn't mean I can't be nervous."

"Last night was fun, wasn't it?"

"It was."

"I like Matt's family. His father's funny."

Matt's dad, Michael McFarland, was an amateur co-median who had performed in and around comedy clubs in the Cleveland area for years. Now in his late sixties, he still put on "shows" for his grandchildren.

He was such a nice man, and so was Matt's mother. It had warmed Shawn's heart to see how both parents had welcomed Lauren into their midst. Last night, at the rehearsal dinner, his mother, Angie, had made a point of sitting next to Lauren, and Shawn had heard the older woman say, "It's going to be so nice for Stacy to have a cousin close to her age living right here in Maple Hills."

Lauren had beamed at Stacy who sat across the table from her. She and Cathy's oldest had hit it off immedi-ately. In fact, they were already best friends and spent hours gossiping on the phone and hanging out at the mall together.

"Your parents are wonderful," Shawn had said wist-fully to Matt when the dinner was over and they were saying good-night.

He'd put his arms around her and held her close for a long moment. "Your parents are here in spirit," he'd said gently.

Her eyes had filled with tears. He always knew what she was feeling. And he always knew exactly what to say to make her feel better.

"Yes," Shawn said now, "his father *is* funny."

"Did you know his mother is a quilter?" Lauren asked.

"Yes, he told me."

"She sells her quilts all over the state."

"I know."

"Guess what she told me?"

Shawn smiled. "I have no idea."

"She said she's going to teach Stacy to quilt. And she said if I was interested, I could come to Cleveland with Stacy and learn, too!"

"And *are* you interested?"

"I think it would be cool."

Recently Shawn had begun to believe in miracles. Because what else could explain her daughter's complete change of heart regarding Matt, whom she now referred to as her "cool" stepdad when talking about him to others?

Finishing her coffee, Shawn tried to decide what she felt like eating. "Want some pancakes?" she said to Lauren.

"Sure."

Decision made, Shawn unearthed the box of pancake mix and began to prepare the batter. Twenty minutes later, she sat down opposite Lauren—a plate of pancakes in front of each. They had just finished eating when the phone rang.

Lauren jumped up. "I'll get it."

It was probably for her, anyway, Shawn thought.

"Oh, hi, Matt," Lauren said. "Um, yeah, she is, but you're not supposed to talk to the bride before the wedding."

"He's not supposed to *see* me, but we can talk to each other," Shawn said.

Lauren rolled her eyes and laughed at something Matt was saying. "Oh, okay. I'll let you talk to her. But only for a minute. She has tons to do to get ready." Laughing, she handed Shawn the phone.

"Good morning," Shawn said.

"Good morning, gorgeous. Did you sleep well?"

Oh, she loved when he talked to her in that sexy voice. "If you're asking if I dreamed of you, the answer is no," she teased.

"I did enough dreaming for both of us," he said in an even sexier voice.

She laughed.

"Just wait till I get you alone tonight."

Shawn glanced up. Lauren was still standing there. "Lauren," she said, "this is an obscene call. Maybe you shouldn't be standing there listening."

At the other end, Matt laughed. "She can't hear me."

"Wanna bet?" Shawn said. "I do have a speaker phone button, you know." After a few seconds, she relented. "But I didn't turn it on."

"Okay, you've had your fun. Now for the reason I called."

"I was wondering when you'd get to the point."

"The point is, I just wanted to tell you that when I woke up this morning, I decided I was the luckiest man in the world."

Shawn smiled. "I feel exactly the same way."

Soon after, Matt said he guessed he'd better let her go so she could start getting ready, and they said goodbye. By the time Shawn and Lauren had cleaned up the kitchen, and both taken their showers, it was almost nine and time for Zoe and Emma to arrive.

Zoe and Lauren were serving as Shawn's only attendants. Lauren as maid of honor, Zoe as a bridesmaid. Emma, who was a whiz at makeup and hair, had volunteered to do the honors for all three.

By ten-twenty, all were ready to go.

"Oh, Shawn," Zoe said when Shawn came downstairs where the others were waiting. "You look beautiful."

Lauren's eyes were shining. "Yeah, Mom, you look beautiful."

Shawn wore a cream-colored, ankle-length lace dress with long sleeves and a deep V-neckline. On her feet were strappy gold sandals. Emma had piled her hair on top of her head and held it in place with pearl-studded combs. Tiny pearl earrings and a delicate diamond tennis bracelet—a thirtieth birthday present from Shawn's parents—completed her bridal outfit. "I think we all look pretty doggone good," Shawn said.

Lauren and Zoe were dressed in complementary shades of apricot and gold. With her clouds of dark hair and soft gray eyes, Emma looked gorgeous in black.

Zoe had hired a limousine to pick them up and take them to the church. When Shawn had protested, saying it was too much money to spend on something so frivolous, Zoe had countered with, "Frivolous! It's not frivolous. You deserve a limousine on your wedding day, Shawn, and I won't hear another word on the subject."

Shawn had to admit it felt pretty good to be riding in such style and comfort.

At the chapel, which Shawn could see was already nearly full, she was hustled into a private room where her and her attendants' flowers were waiting.

While they waited for the signal to leave the room, Lauren fussed with Shawn's hair. "Are you still nervous?"

Zoe snorted. "Of course, she's nervous. As well she should be. Marriage isn't for wimps, you know."

Shawn grinned. Zoe always amused her.

"Mom isn't a wimp," Lauren said.

"Did I say she was?" Zoe countered.

Just then there was a soft knock on the door. "It's time," Emma said, poking her head in.

Five minutes later, Shawn, preceded by Zoe and Lauren, stood in the vestibule of the chapel. Butterflies tickled her stomach as she waited.

Soon she would be Matt's wife. Just the thought sent shivers up her spine.

When the first strains of "Trumpet Voluntary" sounded, Shawn took a deep breath.

Lauren slowly started down the aisle.

A moment later, Zoe followed.

And then it was Shawn's turn.

There was no one to give her away. No one but Lauren, who would answer when the minister asked, so Shawn walked alone toward Matt.

Heads turned as she passed. Low murmurs of appreciation floated in the air as the guests saw her. The scent of roses mixed with the perfume of the women guests and the faint smoke from the many candles burning in the church.

Shawn glided down the aisle as if in a dream. She had eyes only for Matt, who waited for her at the front of the church. He looked so handsome in his dark tux, with his hair slicked back. So handsome and so sweet. Oh, how she loved him!

His father was serving as his best man and his brother, John, was his other groomsman. Both stood behind him as they waited for her.

Reverend Humble, the longtime minister of her church, stood waiting, too, an open book in his hands.

When Shawn drew even with the first pew, she stopped. Matt stepped forward.

"Dearly beloved," Reverend Humble intoned. "We

are gathered together in the sign of God and in the face of this company to join together this man and this woman in holy matrimony."

Matt smiled at Shawn.

"Through marriage," the minister continued, "this man, Matthew Dominick McFarland, and this woman, Shawn Gibson Fletcher, are making a commitment together to face their disappointments, embrace their dreams, realize their hopes, and to accept each other's failures."

He continued to read the traditional introduction, then looked up and said, "Who gives this woman in marriage to this man?"

"I do," Lauren said, walking forward. With eyes suspiciously shiny, she reached for Shawn's hand and placed it in Matt's.

Then she leaned forward and kissed Shawn.

Shawn knew her own eyes were shiny, too. She also knew she had never loved her daughter as much as she did at this moment.

The rest of the ceremony went quickly. Shawn and Matt said their vows and made their promises and exchanged their rings—Shawn's a beautiful circlet of diamonds and Matt's a plain circle of gold.

And then Reverend Humble, smiling, said, "Ladies and gentlemen, I now present to you Mr. and Mrs. Matthew McFarland."

The guests began to clap and there were a few whistles. As Shawn's eyes met Matt's, she decided that she wasn't just the luckiest woman in the world. She was the luckiest woman in the entire universe.

Epilogue

Six months later

Lauren was in the middle of an e-mail to Doug. She had just told him she couldn't wait for summer when the two of them would once again be counselors at the Sunshine Camp.

Everything's so different here now. My dad and Alexandra have been married a year, and my little brother, Jeremy, is already five months old. He's so cute, Doug. I just love him to death. I will really miss him when I'm in college. I'm going to have to come home often.

And guess what! (You'll never guess!) My *mom* is going to have a baby, too! Isn't that cool?

At first, I was kind of embarrassed about her being pregnant, at her age and all, but now I think it's really great. With me going off to college next year, she'll have someone new to fuss over. I hope she has a girl. I'd love to have a little sister.

I am a little worried about my dad, though. I don't think his marriage to Alexandra is going to last. They are fighting a lot. If it wasn't for Jeremy, I wouldn't even like going over there, because it's not much fun. My dad tries, but you can tell he's unhappy, and Alexandra doesn't even try.

You know, my dad really screwed up, but I can't help feeling sorry for him. I think he regrets what happened with my mom, but it's too late. She learned to get along without him, and now she's happier than she ever was before.

Oh, and guess what? My quilt won a blue ribbon at the quilt show last week. I could hardly believe it. Grandma Angie (that's Matt's mother) said she's never seen anyone catch on to quilting as fast I did. I can't believe how much I love it, especially designing the quilts. It's the most fun thing I've ever done. I'm doing a new quilt now. This one is going to be a baby lying on a crescent moon, like it was in a cradle. It's for my mom and the nursery she's planning.

As Lauren signed her name to the e-mail, she kept thinking about her mom and Matt and how happy they were, and then she thought about the new baby coming.

And then, smiling, she began to dream about what it would be like to have a baby of her own. Maybe one with Doug's dimples.

* * * * *

Coming next month—Zoe's story! Look for
IT RUNS IN THE FAMILY, the next book in the
CALLIE'S CORNER CAFÉ series, in February, only
from Patricia Kay and Special Edition.

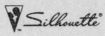

SPECIAL EDITION™

IT RUNS IN THE FAMILY

The second book in *USA TODAY* bestselling author Patricia Kay's lighthearted miniseries

Callie's Corner Café:
It's where good friends meet...

Zoe Madison's fling with a rock star was ancient history, until her daughter, Emma, flew to L.A. to meet the star...and discovered he was her father! Could Zoe protect Emma from her newfound dad's empty Hollywood promises? Maybe, with the help of a special man....

Available February 2006

You can also catch up with the
Callie's Corner Café gang in

A PERFECT LIFE, January 2006
SHE'S THE ONE, March 2006

Where love comes alive™

Visit Silhouette Books at www.eHarlequin.com   SSEIRITF

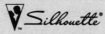

SPECIAL EDITION™

HUSBANDS AND OTHER STRANGERS

by

Marie Ferrarella

A boating accident left Gayle Elliott Conway with amnesia and no recollection of the handsome man who came to her rescue…her husband. Convinced there was more to the story, Taylor Conway set out for answers and a way back into the heart of the woman he loved.

Available February 2006

If you enjoyed what you just read,
then we've got an offer you can't resist!

Take 2 bestselling love stories FREE!

Plus get a FREE surprise gift!

Clip this page and mail it to Silhouette Reader Service™

IN U.S.A.	IN CANADA
3010 Walden Ave.	P.O. Box 609
P.O. Box 1867	Fort Erie, Ontario
Buffalo, N.Y. 14240-1867	L2A 5X3

YES! Please send me 2 free Silhouette Special Edition® novels and my free surprise gift. After receiving them, if I don't wish to receive anymore, I can return the shipping statement marked cancel. If I don't cancel, I will receive 6 brand-new novels every month, before they're available in stores! In the U.S.A., bill me at the bargain price of $4.24 plus 25¢ shipping and handling per book and applicable sales tax, if any*. In Canada, bill me at the bargain price of $4.99 plus 25¢ shipping and handling per book and applicable taxes**. That's the complete price and a savings of at least 10% off the cover prices—what a great deal! I understand that accepting the 2 free books and gift places me under no obligation ever to buy any books. I can always return a shipment and cancel at any time. Even if I never buy another book from Silhouette, the 2 free books and gift are mine to keep forever.

235 SDN DZ9D
335 SDN DZ9E

Name	(PLEASE PRINT)	
Address	Apt.#	
City	State/Prov.	Zip/Postal Code

Not valid to current Silhouette Special Edition® subscribers.

Want to try two free books from another series?
Call 1-800-873-8635 or visit www.morefreebooks.com.

* Terms and prices subject to change without notice. Sales tax applicable in N.Y.
** Canadian residents will be charged applicable provincial taxes and GST.
All orders subject to approval. Offer limited to one per household.
® are registered trademarks owned and used by the trademark owner and or its licensee.

SPED04R   ©2004 Harlequin Enterprises Limited

eHARLEQUIN.com

The Ultimate Destination for Women's Fiction

For FREE online reading, visit
www.eHarlequin.com now and enjoy:

Online Reads
Read **Daily** and **Weekly** chapters from
our Internet-exclusive stories by your
favorite authors.

Interactive Novels
Cast your vote to help decide how these
stories unfold...then stay tuned!

Quick Reads
For shorter romantic reads, try our
collection of Poems, Toasts, & More!

Online Read Library
Miss one of our online reads?
Come here to catch up!

Reading Groups
Discuss, share and rave with other
community members!

For great reading online,
visit www.eHarlequin.com today!

INTONL04R

COMING NEXT MONTH